AF146427

Magical Nights in Marrakesh

Helene Brochett

Magical Nights in Marrakesh

or: How I learned to perceive life with all senses,
while time and space shifted

Bibliographical Information of the Deutsche Nationalbibliothek
This publication is listed in the Deutsche Nationalbibliographie
of the Deutsche Nationalbibliothek; detailed bibliographical
information can be accessed under http: //dnb.d-nb.de

© 2014 Helene Brochett
Printing, Production and Layout: BoD – Books on Demand,
Norderstedt
ISBN: 978-3-7357-7728-7

Contents

Immersing Into Another World   7

Feeling Images and Colours   21

Moving With the Rhythm of the Masses   46

Venturing into the New   67

Crossing Boundaries   81

Stars Within Reach   101

A New Life Begins   115

Immersing Into Another World

The plane landed with a jolt, braked sharply and slowly rolled to a standstill. We stopped approximately about hundred meters from the terminal. Greeted by hot and dry air Marianne and I stepped out onto the gangway. I was thrown into this world as if I had stepped through a wall. The sky was purple and opalescent light reached us through a thin haze.

At the arrival desk we were faced with a long wait. Everything was stalling. Having received the passports, the inspectors typed something into their computers and proceeded to wait endlessly before handing the documents back with a nod, approving the entry. Some people became agitated about the procedure. Marianne and I remained unfazed, watching with mild amusement the rush some people seemed to have at the beginning of their holiday. Yet, soon enough, even I became nervous and agitated because once we had left passport control behind us; the search for my suitcase at the baggage claim was unsuccessful. All the other passengers from our plane had hauled their luggage off the conveyor belt, but mine remained elusive. At first I was unable to locate any service personnel to complain about my missing property. I was worried that someone else had inadvertently – or even purposely – taken my suitcase. What's more, Marianne and I were worried that the taxi driver who had been sent by our guest house to pick us up would drive off without us, as he might assume that we hadn't arrived. So Marianne went outside to make sure he waited while I attempted to solve the issue of my missing suitcase.

Finally, after knocking on every door in the arrivals area and asking several people who were responsible for the luggage inspection, I found two airline personnel. Communicating with them proved somewhat difficult as they initially pretended not to understand me, although my English and French are rather passable. When I became increasingly annoyed by their ignorance I quite harshly insisted on a written report of my loss, and finally, they obliged. Despite all my cursing and describing the problems I would face without my luggage, the suitcase remained missing, and they were unable to tell me whether it got lost in transit, or whether it had been stolen from the conveyor belt. They promised to contact me in my hotel if their enquiries were in any way successful.

Angry and flustered I rushed off with my hand luggage to catch up with Marianne. After all that mess we finally left the airport in our taxi – a full one and a half hours after we had landed. On the way into town we saw that everything was still tinted with the purple colour we had first noticed when we left the plane. It felt as if I was in a surreal world, illuminated by unnatural light sources. I was reminded of one of James Turrell's light creations.

We drove down a straight four-lane road lined with palm trees and flowerbeds. After a while we passed a vast, modern holiday estate that still had some unfinished areas. The already completed buildings had all been painted in an antique pink that shone like the towering single facet of a huge pale ruby. A bit further on we saw huge mansions hidden behind long walls. These also had been painted with that antique pink. The evening sun illuminated some of the surfaces and turned them into crimson. All this enhanced the illusion of an alternate reality. The houses featured flat roofs, archways, pillars and balconies all the way round. They were overgrown with flowers and green plants, and some palm trees grew in between them. The shutters were all firmly closed to protect the houses from the sun and the heat. We didn't get a glimpse of the life in those houses.

Later, large olive trees and orchards lined the road. The orchards were fenced in and lined with irrigation ditches. Once we got closer to the city, the road passed through densely populated districts. The street cafes were full, and many people were milling about. Women with their children trailing dragged heavy carrier bags into their homes or into the next shop. And there was dust. Everywhere.

We crossed several junctions and various roundabouts advancing further into the city. Long walls appeared periodically to our left and right. Behind them, houses were huddled together. The loam rendering here was beige or grey in colour. Again, the evening sun painted everything in warm, glowing hues. Women wandered around by the walls with their children, sometimes in larger groups. Other women casually strolled down a path along the wall, talking, while their children were happily playing. Only very few men were to be seen. Obviously, this was the evening meeting point for the women of the district.

Approaching a junction with palm trees in its centre we saw several national flags of Morocco fluttering in the wind. Traffic was heavier here and needed to be regulated by a policeman. By now the yellow street lanterns had been lit, and the purple and crimson light across the sky faded into dusk.

We turned into a small street. To our left, we saw a high, uneven wall with reddish grey loam rendering. Two-storey houses without windows lined the street. Donkey carts, mopeds, bicycles, trucks and rickety cars drove through the narrow streets and were all over the place. Some carried vegetables, and we watched them being unloaded at several places. Others were laden with furniture, while yet others had rubble piled up high above their rims. Massive amounts of stones were transported on old carts, and the vehicles looked as if they were about to collapse under their weight. In between all that, people rushed through the streets, emerging from shops and yards. Craftsmen had their shops set up on the ground floors of the buildings, and we saw carpenters and metal workers plying their trade. Hustle and bustle was everywhere. Looking into several small windows and doors we saw lamps and candles, and a sense of organized chaos with floors, tables and wash basins all piled up to the ceilings.

Through the open window of our taxi, the noises of this stir rang in our ears. A cacophony of voices, shouts, cries, rattling, blowing horns and hammering washed over us. Sometimes, our taxi driver would curse as other road users proved to be a hindrance, or he would simply shout at passers-by or other drivers from inside the car. Between the houses to our right a tiny alley branched away, and all one could see were high walls at its end. Either, these alleys ended at those walls or they veered off at a right angle. On the left was a high wall with a big gate, and large gold letters announced that it led to the "Lycée Mohammed V".

Suddenly, our taxi driver stopped after what had seemed to be an endless drive through the medina, the historic town centre. From the shadows of an alley a young man with a hand cart approached the taxi. The driver and the young man greeted each other by slapping the other's shoulders. Our luggage was transferred from the taxi to the hand cart, and the young man asked us to follow him into the dark alley past the two-storey houses.

Debris and donkey dung were on the ground. The stench was horrible, and water was dripping from a pipe. Children sat in front of a plain door, while even more children played in another side alley, screeching loudly. Two lanterns offered a dim light. The whole atmosphere was rather eerie, and I felt uneasy thinking that I had to spend the next few days in this area. I wondered what I had gotten myself into and what was waiting for me. At the end of the alley stood a high red brick wall which was in total contrast to the grey decrepit houses of this area. The stones were offset, showing a zigzag pattern, and they were illuminated in order to bring out the shading. A lacquered massive wooden door studded with steel nails was very prominent in the centre of the wall. A sign had been mounted to the left of the door, and yellow straight letters on dark blue ground announced: "Riad Noga". Our guide rang the doorbell, and after a short wait the door opened gently. We entered, and a young man greeted us in French: "Bon soir, Mesdames, bienvenue!" Slowly, we moved along while gaping at the new, enchanting world that was unfolding in front of us. After passing through all the narrow roads, the dirt and the stench, we had now arrived in what can only be described as an idyllic location that seemed to stem from a fairytale.

The months and weeks before our departure had been very stressful for me. I was forced to add new tasks to my responsibilities and had been permanently on the road. At least once a week I had to travel to various cities in Germany in order to meet customers, negotiate contracts or transact business. Sometimes I had been away from home for days on end. During the remaining few days in my office I had to delegate the tasks within my team and clear all that work that I hadn't been able to finish through our company's network while I was travelling. More often than not I had to plough through hundreds of mails in the morning that were cluttering my inbox. I had to get up early for my work travels in order to catch the first plane or train. Travelling home in the evening usually brought me home late. Taking a nap on the train was never enough to relax or recover properly. On the contrary, I felt that my neck and shoulders deteriorated because my head always fell forward when I nodded off. Even lying in bed, my neck was still uptight. I had functioned like clockwork, and all my strength had been consumed by concentrating on my job and its requirements. The last thing I had on my mind was to be away from home during my holiday.

My husband had very much the same problems, albeit for different reasons. His business was stalling. He had ordered a new range of articles, and his storage was full up, yet there were no customers to buy the wares. The loans for the working funds were suffocating him, he had to find money to pay his employees, and new marketing strategies cost additional money. He became increasingly nervous and irritable, and soon he spent more time than ever before in his shop. At home, he would only brood over his business papers. As I was away a lot of the time, we hardly found any time to talk to each other – let alone for some tender love and care. We were far too absorbed in our professional matters and merely coexisted.

When my friend asked me whether I could accompany her to Marrakesh, I initially wanted to decline. What was I supposed to do in a foreign town in Morocco? I needed time for myself and my marriage, provided I was able to get some time off for a holiday. I had been looking forward to sleeping in, enjoying our wonderful flat, reading a thrilling book, cooking something delicious with my husband and eating it with a nice glass of wine. But Marianne didn't relent. She had intended to go to Marrakesh with her longstanding life partner to boost their relationship that had been heading towards a crisis. Unfortunately, they had separated three weeks before the journey. She was adamant to get over the separation and wanted to set forth on that journey, but she didn't want to go alone. She pestered me persistently, until she finally persuaded me to go with her about one week prior to the holiday. My husband also encouraged me to go and said: "Before you continue to work yourself into the ground, and I have to suffer the stress as well, you should go and get some rest and relaxation. I will continue to attempt finding a solution for my business problems. Keep your friend company and look after yourself for a change".

So I switched a few dates and took one week off. Changing the flight's booking to my name was no problem, and the guest house didn't care who shared Marianne's room. I had no time to properly prepare myself for this journey; I didn't even have time to buy some books about Morocco and Marrakesh, let alone read anything about it. The night before our departure I spent literally up until the last minute packing as I had spent the evening in the office, distributing orders and getting contracts ready for signing. Once we settled into our seats on the plane, I took a deep breath – and made myself comfortable to sleep.

We had to change planes in Madrid, and it took up all of our two hours stay to get from one terminal to the other. I was impressed by the terminal where we arrived: Large concrete pillars carrying v-shaped steel beams supported the wave-depicting roof of a seemingly endless hall. The sub construction was lined with wooden poles adding to the illusion of waves. The steel beams had been painted yellow, orange, and red, and they both marked and separated the various terminal areas. I was impressed and regarded everything in detail. The indirect light of modern lamps reflecting their light to the ceiling also enhanced the image of waves. As it was mid-afternoon the artificial light was nonessential though as huge glass windows on both sides allowed the Spanish sun to flood the hall with her light. The unhindered view out onto the runway and its surroundings was breathtaking. The protruding roof and a good climate control made for a comfortable ambience.

The rush and haste of the numerous arriving and departing passengers was slightly alleviated by the generous architecture. This was an enormous achievement of modern architecture which outclassed any of the terminals I had previously encountered in Germany.

At the airport I took a closer look at our flight ticket from Madrid to Marrakesh, wondering about the arrival and departure times. Despite being on a two-hour flight we would arrive in Marrakesh earlier than our time of departure. When I properly thought about it I realised of course that the time difference was responsible for that. Retrospectively I think that the two hours we gained on that day had been an omen for what was awaiting me. I was – that's the way I look at it today – literally thrown into another time on that day. The change of my outlook on life, the tide of new impressions and the questioning of reality would from now on accompany me on my journey.

This was Marianne's and my first visit to Marrakesh and Morocco. We had promised each other before we set off that we would not talk about the problems that had been bothering us before our holiday; we wanted to commit ourselves completely to Marrakesh. And so, we stood full of expectations in the Riad Noga. The German owner greeted us just as friendly a manner as her employees had earlier, and we were ushered to an alcove with lavish settees covered in white linen upholstery. We received a welcome drink and looked around, still in awe.

After a while I realised that we were in a square, beautiful inner yard. I was mesmerized by taking in my new surroundings and tried to memorise everything. Cosy lit lounges were on two sides of the yard; one boasted a large dining table, the other was furnished with sofas. The broad wooden doors leading into these rooms stood wide open. Three trees grew in the yard. Their canopies rose up above the first floor. Climbers covered the walls from the base to the top, while banana plants, palm trees and blossoming bushes grew in huge clay pots and bowls. The surface of the floor was covered in turquoise and blue glazed tiles. The pattern and colour of the floor tiles was repeated in a moulding that sat half way up on one of the calcimined walls. A shallow bowl filled with water stood on a small stand in the centre of the yard, pink and red petals floating in the water. Next to the bowl was a metal cage housing a frequently squawking parrot.

Lanterns and mounted lights illuminated the scene mystically. A roofed but otherwise open gallery spanned three walls on the first floor. Beneath the trees were three steel tables with mosaic tops, ringed with chairs beset with white linen cushions. The corners of the alcove where we sat housed two standard lamps with bulbous ceramic bases, and a wooden table covered in carvings dominated in its centre. Three large colourful paintings decorated the walls. Contrary to the heat we had experienced at the airport and during out journey into town, the temperature in this inner yard was pleasantly cool.

After a brief conversation we were led to our rooms. We passed an archway into a second inner yard with a large swimming pool. It was also lined with turquoise tiles and framed by a blue-tiled rim. Bright spot lights embedded in the lower part of the pool wall were illuminating the water. Several rooms led out onto the yard; those on the first floor were all connected by a roofed gallery. The walls had been painted dark red, while ledges and pillars boasted contrasting yellow ochre. Across from the archway stood a sofa with white linen sheets, and a bar made from dark wood. Both were covered by an arced roof. A large mirror above the sofa reflected the turquoise of the water. Lavish palm trees and green plants grew in large terracotta pots here as well. Everything was enchantingly illuminated by brass lanterns.

We were directed to the red room on the first floor, which was apparently our room. It was presumably called the red room because the walls had been covered in a red, slightly shiny plaster. Red cotton covers interwoven with black and bright threads, as well as many large and small cushions of the same colours graced the bed. The bathroom also featured the red colour of the main room's walls. A rounded, plastered wall served as a partition for the shower. The wardrobes in the room were made of cedar that had been stained in a dark colour. The floor consisted of irregular, dull stones covered with colourful carpets made from natural fibres.

It was comfortable, and we felt at ease straight away. All the furniture had been chosen lovingly and tastefully, and each detail went hand in hand with the others. Several halogen lamps working independently of each other illuminated the walls, or the ceiling, or served as reading lamps at the bedside. We tried them several times just like little children would. Bathrobes and leather slippers had been put out for us. Next to the bed were octagonal bedside tables, and little bowls with sweet snacks had been left as complementary welcome presents. It didn't take us long to discover these deliciously-smelling cookies were made from almonds and honey. A clay pot containing nuts, dates and raisins waited on the desk. Marianne quickly unpacked all that she needed, as I had only the clothes that I was wearing. We freshened up ready for the dinner that was about to begin.

We were invited to the roof terrace for dinner. Climbing up a small stairway with a thick metal handrail we reached the second floor where dining tables had been set up on three different levels. Brick-built benches with rough dark woollen blankets stood by the walls. Even up here there were lavish plants. Dim lights hung in small niches of the wall. We briefly looked down onto the warmly lit alleys that surrounded the house. We could see the pool in the yard of our guest house. From our higher vantage point, the turquoise colour was even more intense. I felt as if I was looking down from a cliff onto a vast, turquoise ocean. We could see the occasional lights from other rooftop gardens and illuminated spires everywhere above the sea of rooftops – the minarets of mosques, as we soon found out. A slight breeze blew. We sat down, still filled with awe. Other guests had almost finished their dinner and were preparing to enjoy their desserts.

As soon as we sat down, an indefinable – at least for us – loud sound began floating through the air. At first I believed it to be a siren, and thought of a fire alarm. But very soon we realised that the muezzins in the mosques had started their call for prayer, and it was these prayers that were being emitted through loudspeakers. I had never heard anything like it before. It sounded like a conversation. Soon, the drawn-out chanting could be heard coming from all sides, multiple magical echoes of the same tone of voice. It was like a concert with many voices. As I read in a book later – and finally understood – it said: "Allahu akbar", "God is great". I really had arrived in a different world. Everything felt beyond-the-real, and I wondered whether I had stepped into one of my nostalgia-filled childhood movies, or into the oriental fairytale I used to listen to frequently on a vinyl record.

The food was delicious. We had ordered a Moroccan salad and a tajine. Moroccan salad consists of chopped tomatoes, cucumbers and onions with aromatic herbs, vinegar and oil. The tajine is a flat, round ceramic pot with a cone-shaped lid, and the dishes derive their name from it. Inside this pot, vegetables and meat are being cooked above a charcoal fire. Our tajine consisted of chicken with marinated lemon, and of course oriental spices such as the indispensable cumin. All this was served with fresh white bread. Dessert consisted of pomegranate seeds that had been dressed with a slightly sweet juice. We drank rosé wine with our meal.

Just short of midnight we slumped into our bed, tired yet still churned up inside. I had decided to put the problem with my suitcase out of my mind, and didn't want to be angry about it anymore. When I dozed off I had the feeling that crossing the threshold of this guest house had delivered me into a new life, just as I had imagined as a child. I remembered seeing images in my dreams during my childhood just before I woke up. Back then I imagined that I would be a totally different person in another life when I awoke. I envisioned that I was all grown up, and all the worries that I was familiar with from my parents as they were fighting for the livelihood for our large family had faded. This feeling, as if I was dreaming a dream within a dream, came back to me while I fell asleep on this first night in Marrakesh.

Feeling Images and Colours

I slept soundly that night. In the morning, I heard birds twittering, quietly at first but gradually increasing in volume. While I slowly woke up I looked out to see the red, crumbling walls and the dark, creepy alleys around us. It felt strange being woken up by birds in this kind of environment, and it also seemed to be far too early at six in the morning. That was owed to the time difference, according to my inner rhythm it was eight already. I moved about quietly as my friend was still fast asleep. I glimpsed into the inner yard. Another couple was just about to jump into the pool. The water splashed gently. This morning was too chilly for my liking to go swimming though. So I grabbed yesterday's newspaper that I had taken from the airplane, wrapped myself into the bathrobe and went to the roof terrace. Gentle sunlight greeted me. The day was about to begin.

I took a look around in the first daylight. The air was now fresh and clear, unlike last night. From the rooftop garden you looked at a vast ocean of houses and roofs and many, many roof terraces. Some roofs were covered in debris and rubbish; others boasted gardens and were green just like the one I stood on. Yet others featured strange structures and I wondered whether they were used to warm up water. An army of satellite dishes had been mounted onto the roofs. In between the houses some scrawny palm trees poked out above the roofs. A bit further in the west towered large green conifers, palm branches and cypresses. Maybe there was a park over there. I could hear a cock crowing from another yard. Slowly, footsteps fell in the alleys. Behind the roofs, almost close enough to touch them, a mountain range rose up. That had to be Atlas, the roof of Africa!

I didn't get a chance to read more than the newspaper's headlines. I was far too distracted by looking around. Another rooftop garden obviously also belonged to the guest house. It featured a gazebo made of dark wooden poles, and an upholstered suite with white linen. Both rooftop gardens were furnished with tables, benches, deckchairs and sunshades. In between the buildings bulged a dome made from stone, its peak decorated with three metal orbs on top of each other looking like a replica of a mosque. The roof ridges were lined with blue, half-rounded roof tiles. The stairway leading up to the roof terrace was shielded by a small square roof, also covered in blue tiles. In the morning light the red and orange wall colour appeared to be totally different than it did in darkness. The plants were more readily recognisable and I identified bougainvilleas, olive trees, palm trees, geraniums and colourful nettles. Below the rooftop garden grew large Benjamin's figs and fichus trees. In between, large red hibiscus blossoms stuck out. This abundance of plants was soothing and heady among all the bleak walls and the other roofs.

After a while, two young men began laying the tables for breakfast. Blue and red ornamented ceramics were placed as tableware for breakfast. Small bowls looking like tajines stood on large wooden plates, featuring the same patterns and colours as the rest of the tableware. I picked up the lids and discovered that they contained butter, marmalade, date puree, honey and cereals. Freshly squeezed orange juice, lovely smelling coffee and peppermint tea were available, as well as baguette, flatbread, fried eggs, omelette and cheese.

One by one the guests arrived for breakfast. Marianne had also appeared and was just as amazed as I was by the view. After an extensive breakfast we asked for leaflets and a guide so we could plan our day. First of all I told the lady of the house about my luggage troubles and she promised to make some inquiries with the airline. I decided to buy some essential clothes for the next two days during our walk through town.

Our first destination was the Jemaa el-Fnaa, which means something like the "Assembly of Death". All travel guides stated that this was a *must* for every visit to Marrakesh, and that most of the city's life took place here. According to the map we had to cross this square anyway on our way to the souks – as the market halls, or even the bazaar are called – the museums and the stops for sightseeing tours.

We had been dawdling for quite a while and finally left in the latter hours of the morning, armed with a road map of the medina. We walked down a long alley from our house to a small square. In broad daylight we realised that some of the high house walls did have small windows with embellished metal bars after all. A child pressed his face against the metal bars on the upper floor attempting to get a glimpse of what was happening in the alley.

Many cars were parked on the small square. People on bicycles and mopeds zigzagged around us and the other passers-by. Craft businesses and shops were set up in the ground floors of the surrounding houses. As I had noticed the night before, most of them had barely enough room for a chair as they were otherwise crammed with wares. A cyber café was located right next to all these medieval looking businesses as if it was the most natural thing in the world. In a gateway to a yard, CDs and DVDs had been lined up on a rickety table. Loud, blasting music was supposed to attract customers. The square was covered in cobblestones, but a large pothole gaped on the right side. Dust and dirt were whirling up. At the end of the square we had to turn into another narrow alley. The cobbles here had also been turned up, and all the stones had been piled up. A water pipe protruded from the ground, followed the road for a few meters and then disappeared again into another hole. The ground was wet as the pipe was leaking water everywhere. All passersby, be they on mopeds, or with hand carts or donkeys, had to balance around the potholes and over the pile of stones. It didn't matter whether people wore freshly cleaned shoes or slippers, whether they had to squeeze past the bottle neck near the building site, or whether they had to wait in the mud or on top of the stone pile – all of them walked imperturbably through the puddles, the dirt and the dust as if it was nothing unusual.

The alleys that followed were so narrow that cars were unable to pass through them. They were also lined with old houses, some of them seemed derelict. Dirty, puny doors led into these houses. Now and then we would pass a neat door; one of them even had a beautiful frame made of tiles.

We turned right and found ourselves in a small business street crowded with little shops on both sides. Everything we could possibly imagine was being sold in these shops. Carpets, clothing, decorative fabrics, jewellery, shoes, TV appliances, telephones, vegetables, pastries, metal lamps, lanterns, pottery, washing detergents – simply everything. In between, hair dressers, tailors, carpenters, leather workers and dentists offered their services. There were laundries and telecommunication shops, a cinema, a mosque, a beauty care shop, a pharmacist and a hamam, which is what we call a Turkish bath. It was pandemonium. The floors of several businesses consisted of marble, while others were very old, dirty and dusty. Some shops displayed their wares decoratively in windows; others had their stands blocking the alleys. Everywhere clothes dangled hanging from marquees and canopies. The marquees were very varied as well. Some of them were old plastic tarpaulins covered in dirt, feebly attempting to protect shops and wares alike from the sun and from bleaching. Others were brand-new, displaying advertising slogans.

Some merchants stood outside their shops, trying to invite us to stop and browse, while others haggled with customers or sat sleepily on the steps to the entrances. Low passageways led to even more workshops and alleys in between the houses. Tourists and locals milled about in this confined space. Some people casually strolled along while others purposefully strode ahead. In between them, there were yet more people with mopeds, bicycles, donkey carts and hand carts. We were faced with incredible pushing and shoving. We sometimes had to leap to one side in order to avoid moped riders. They raced towards the crowd with unbelievable speed and we were scared that we might get hit. Young guys rode these mopeds, while veiled girls or stylish women with modern clothes and fancy hairstyles sat on the back seat. We even saw a black-veiled woman riding a rickety moped past us.

The attires of the Moroccans that passed us were also very varied. Modern men and women dressed in Western-style T-shirts and jeans were quite common. Many people simply wore a djellaba – a garment made of wool – and the ever popular light, flat open-back slippers – the babouches – despite the fact that you had to shuffle along wearing those, else they might slip off your feet. Veiled women walked next to revealingly dressed girls. Begging, many of them elderly women, held out their hands or huddled in corners. The diversity and variety we encountered during our fifteen-minute walk was unbelievable. Suddenly, the Jemaa el-Fnaa unfolded before us.

The square was surrounded by cafes and shops. We couldn't determine how far it stretched. To one side we saw rooftop cafes with opened sunshields, while huge bright red and orange carpets hung from the roof ridges of the other side, obviously serving as advertisements for carpet merchants. Newsagents and souvenir shops had set up little stalls right next to the shops and cafes. The mixture of tourists, pedestrians, merchants, snake charmers, water vendors and shoeblacks was even more vibrant there. Men and women wrapped in djellabas sat on tiny stools but we couldn't determine what they were selling. Yet more men and women sat on the floor with a cloth spread out next to them offering various items from second hand mobile phones to herbs and sweets. One merchant had piled up numerous false teeth on his cloth, offering them for sale in all earnest.

The smell of incense wafted across the square at one point. Carts with small sunshields had oranges piled up on their load area, and freshly squeezed orange juice was offered to order.

We strolled around, and several times people badgered us, wanting to sell their wares. Moped riders almost bumped into us on more than a few occasions, so we finally settled into one of the cafes with a view of the square to get some rest. From here we were able to see several large buildings on the far side of the square: the "Banque Al-Maghrib" that resided in a representative building, the magnificent post office and some public offices flying the Moroccan flag. In between those the "Club Med" was located behind a large wall. Flute players and drummers caused a musical raucous on the square, while merchants called out their wares and prices. This colourful chaos felt straining to us after the tranquillity of our Riad. We ordered a thè à la menthe, the mandatory peppermint tea, and mused for a while. Marianne wanted to post a letter that she had forgotten about and went to the post office. I stayed on the café patio wondering whether I should find this city attractive or repulsive. All those impressions that had been assailing me since our arrival were contrasting, and I found them confusing.

At the table next to me sat a very cultured, European-looking woman with grey hair, wearing a light grey linen costume. The small red cloth that was tied around her neck created a lovely contrast. She had apparently noticed us earlier, and after a while she approached me and greeted me in German. The expression on my face and my demeanour must have betrayed the way I felt. We started talking. She told me that she lived in Marrakesh for most of the year, the remainder of the time she spent in Europe. When I told her where we lived in the medina, she replied that it had been a very wise move to have our accommodation in a Riad since that would leave us in the centre of everything. She continued: "All those finding accommodation in the elegant hotels or apartments on the outskirts of town will never experience life in Marrakesh as immediate as someone in a Riad will. Marrakesh has a very special charm that you will find nowhere else in the world. But you will have to experience that charm for yourself." She suddenly became very serious and spoke to me emphatically, "Walk through this city with your eyes and ears open. Try to take in all the smells, even if they are disgusting, and let the emotions that will befall you run their course. Don't give up too early. Marrakesh is not just what you think you see, hear, smell or feel. Marrakesh holds a secret for everyone. Yet you have to discover yours for yourself". She bid me goodbye, claiming she had almost forgotten an appointment. Just before she left, she whispered to me that we would surely meet again during my stay.

I was confused, puzzled and also curious, mulling her words over again. How was I supposed to understand that *special charm* or even find out a secret about myself? I didn't really feel like embarking on esoteric adventures. I just wanted to be out and about with my friend and hopefully get some well-deserved rest. We had given all the storytellers and fortune-tellers on Jemaa el-Fnaa who promised you the world for just a few Dirham a wide berth, presuming that they wouldn't be able to communicate with us in a language that we understood. All holiday enthusiasm aside, we intended to stay firmly grounded in reality.

Although this conversation had been exciting and had left me pensive, I didn't feel the urge to tell Marianne about it when she returned, and so I kept it to myself. We decided to continue our scouting mission through the medina and the souks.

The souks are vast market halls with large, closely placed stalls. Small bars with rush mats shield the aisles between them. We read in our city guide that the shops were separated into handicrafts and trade. All goods were produced and sold here. We found carpenters, carvers, tapestry makers, carpet vendors, blacksmiths, cobblers, lamp manufacturers, basket weavers, and jewellery and leather merchants. Hammering and clanking assaulted our ears from all sides. The diversity and the multitudinous teeming crowd were almost too much for us. Small alleys branched off the main aisles, only to fork into even smaller alleys. Some of the shops would extend into backrooms that were hidden from view. We were overwhelmed by the colours. Red and orange hues were extremely prominent. Everything was readily available, and the sheer range and mixture was beyond anything we had ever seen. Next to modern or traditional fabrics, carpets, leather, iron and clay goods, there were beautifully adorned ceramic bowls, baskets, wicker furniture, gold and silver jewellery, semiprecious stones, watches, fashion jewellery and perfumes being offered. Merchants, women and children stood in between all of these, selling baked goods from huge baking trays. Meat skewers or chickens were being fried and piled up sky-high next to shops exhibiting the finest silk and damask. We had no idea who was supposed to buy and eat all that. Spice racks had been placed between those piles. Spices we had never even heard of were being sold here along with saffron, curcuma and cumin. Large bunches of herbs dangled from ceilings. Dried herbs such as lavender, thyme, rosemary and cloves welled forth from big sacks in front of the market stalls. Other stalls offered various dates and dried fruit, as well as all sorts of olives.

Initially, we stopped to gander at the products, but after a while, we were not quite so impressed. We weren't able to take in much more and many things just made us nervous, as even here many people were out an about and didn't stop short of trying to squeeze mopeds, bicycles, donkey carts and burden bearers through the narrow aisles. They squeezed past, apologised and rushed along but they hardly bumped into one another. The pungent fumes emitted by the mopeds spread among the people, and they covered spices and natural goods alike. In some areas, repulsive stenches insulted our noses and we tried to hurry past them. We could smell fish remains, rotting meat, urine, decay and refuse. Outside the perfume shops, however, we inhaled the lovely aromas of rose water, lavender and bergamot.

Every merchant tried to find customers and hoped that screaming out especially low prices would attract pedestrians. False guides mingled with the crowd in order to entice tourists to certain shops or stalls. We were faced with so many new impressions that we felt like being in a sensual frenzy.

After a while we left the bazaar behind us and emerged onto a small square with even more market stalls. These were smaller and not quite as spectacular. Those in the middle were paltry. Colourful carpets hung from the walls of houses roofs, which indicated that many carpet merchants were here. But we also noticed many leather goods on display in this area. Out here, even bigger bunches of spices and herbs were on offer than inside the souks. We saw all kinds of curious items such as small cedar wood sticks with cotton strips wrapped around them. Dried, squashed lizards and hedgehogs were lined up on small tables as if someone had scraped them off the streets. Living iguanas, toads, squirrels and turtles were being kept in small cages. The iguanas and lizards seemed dozy, or they were half-dead already, while the squirrels playfully jumped around in their small cages. This was obviously a market for all sorts of natural cures, aphrodisiacs and animistic items. It appeared to be an Eldorado for quacks.

Several merchants sprayed water onto the dry, loamy ground in an attempt to bind some of the dust and to generate a bit of coolness from the moist. We had to avoid puddles repeatedly, and our shoes were even dirtier than they would have been from just the dust. A tea salon with Coca Cola sunshields on top of a roof provided another beautiful view down onto the market life. We drank a mineral water here, and once we had seen enough, we took a side road to the "Musée de Marrakesh" and the "Medersa Ben Youssef", which is a Quran school and high school for theology and law that has been around for many centuries.

The Medersa is situated between closely huddled houses with long, bare walls. A broad, richly adorned wooden gate allows access. We walked through a long, dark passageway and entered a large inner courtyard with a shallow, rectangular water basin at its centre. Three alcoves lined with geometric ornaments and mosaics consisting of small tiles opened up into the courtyard on the right, left and far side. The colours blue, turquoise and white were predominant here. Their high ceilings featured opulently carved wooden beams; the connecting bars had been painted in rich colours. Openwork fences made from dark wood panels with carvings defined the alcoves from the yard. As the air circulated below the ceilings, it felt refreshingly cool. The alcove entrances boasted opulent ornaments and arabesques that were either carved into the plaster or fixed as stucco. The floor was covered in marble, and walking on it seemed to muffle the sound of your footsteps.

We looked up to the first floor and saw large windows made of dark wood that had been crested with openwork carvings as well. This place was tranquil and sublime, and the solemn atmosphere prompted visitors to move quietly and slowly. Many sat down on the wicker chairs provided, pausing and taking in the unobtrusive beauty of the ornaments and the rooms.

From the exit, two stairways led up to the first floor, where we could visit the former dormitories of the Quran pupils and students. We sensed that this had been a perfect environment for religious studies and praying. It was in the centre of the historic town, yet far away from the hustle and bustle of the markets, and we felt tranquil and reverent.

Only a few steps away from the Medersa sat the museum of Marrakesh. A vast plaza surrounded by many other large buildings, including a mosque, stretched out in front of it.

The outer walls of the museum had been restored, and a modern cafe was located in the yard. We heard oriental sounding music mixed with pop music elements. The walls here were also adorned with beautiful mosaics with small ceramic tiles forming blossoms and rosettes. Large, intricately crested iron and brass lanterns were everywhere in the sheltered yard. They even dwarfed the magnificent chandeliers that we are used to from European castles. The side rooms were furnished in the characteristic fashion for these Berber houses, and they also housed long benches with thick, embroidered cushions. The Berber are renowned for their handicrafts, and typical carpets, clothes and jewellery were on show. Despite the building's splendour and the interesting exhibits, we could see a certain degree of decay and couldn't help but notice certain morbidity. We took a different route through the medina on our way back.

We had a road map showing a plethora of roads but only a few of them featured street names. After brief consideration we opted for following our instincts and set off in an appropriate direction. The alleys in this part of the medina were also narrow with high, windowless walls. Some houses were almost in ruins and it didn't look as if people were still living in them. Still, when we passed one of the doors of such a ruin, a modern styled woman emerged. In between these ruins we passed some neat and well-maintained houses, judging by their walls, the front door and their rooftop gardens that we could see from the ground. Sometimes there were more pedestrians in these alleys, sometimes less. Some shuffled along, others hastened past us. Women led their children by the hand, or had them tied onto their backs while walking through the streets. One woman walked past us with the baking tray full of flatbreads that she had covered with a cloth.

Some people in this quarter were also clad in the traditional djellaba – which basically looks like a long nightgown – while others were dressed in a more European way. We saw women veiled from head to toe, women and girls with headscarves and woman wearing no headdress at all. All these different ways of dressing coexisted as a matter of course. Yet even in this district we still had difficulties evading the mopeds and bicycle riders.

The alleys were contorted, additional passageways suddenly forked off and sometimes we were unable to discern our main direction. To begin with, the alleys we walked through were somewhat boring, but as we progressed we found shops on the ground floors. Telecommunication shops and cyber cafés for people who don't own a telephone or internet connection at home were commonplace. Chemists, pharmacies and dentists – specialists in pulling teeth, although they cannot be compared to our Western dental practitioners – were everywhere in between. Various craftsmen worked in back yards. Several young men fastened thin, more than ten meter long threads along the house walls and aroused our curiosity. We had no explanation for what they were doing and found out several days later that they were silk spoolers. The silken threads were being used to embroider djellabas.

We had great difficulties finding our way through this labyrinth as there were no street names anywhere to be seen. Even had the names been marked on the map, they would have been no use to us under these circumstances. The houses were packed tightly together, and all you could see was the sky up above. Distinctive buildings of the city that would have provided some kind of orientation were nowhere to be seen. Sometimes, we ended up in front of a wall or a house entrance – we had walked into a dead end. That meant we had to double back to the point where we assumed we had lost our way.

We crossed several small squares. Every time we encountered a different environment. An official building stood on one of the squares. Moroccan flags fluttered in the wind and two policemen stood idly in front of it. Benches had been placed under scrawny trees, and elderly people chatted or snoozed in the shade. Several mobile vendors sold fruit and vegetables from the loading area of their carts. Decaying fruit, vegetable leftovers and carrier bags littered the floor. There was a powerful stench of mould, decay and fish. We could but wonder how anyone could sell groceries in these unhygienic conditions. To us that was unthinkable.

Another square was surrounded by shops with many different wares. Furniture, mattresses, upholstery and wicker was being manufactured and sold. There was also clothing, carpets, small wares, toys, mobile phones, cosmetics – and right next to them … daggers. We saw just about everything. Everything we cram into our large department stores is sold separately here in different shops. Each merchant has picked a corner for his business, and a special offer.

Often these shops were so tiny and rammed so full of wares that the merchants hardly had enough room for themselves.

After the previous, quieter alleys, we were back to a square with chaos, bustle, screaming and music. Suddenly and totally unexpectedly a driver of a large black and polished car drove through the crowd and demanded that people got out of his way. How did he manage to reach the historic town centre with that car? Most of the alleys were far too narrow for these kinds of cars. So far we hadn't seen any cars in the historic town centre apart from some small trucks transporting goods.

We turned into a small road where most people were headed. Finally, we saw the first road sign and it informed us that this was Rue Dabachi. As this road was also marked on our map, we finally had some orientation. Unfortunately we still didn't know whether we were heading in the right direction. We stopped thinking about it, and several young men approached us. They offered to lead us to the large square, the Jemaa el-Fnaa. We were worried that they might lead us to some shop where we were going to be pestered about buying carpets or jewellery for ridiculous prices. We had been warned about situations like that. It was annoying and it took us quite a while to get rid of them … which we did by simply walking away.

Rue Dabachi appeared to be some kind of main shopping street as we saw even more shops than before. Meat and fish were sold at open stalls. We realised quickly that poor people from the medina were shopping here. Some of the offered goods were so pitiful and stinted that we found it surprising they were offered for sale at all. In some places herbs, fruits and vegetables were spread out on cloths on the ground, and the dust that had been whirled up from passing mopeds settled on the food. Donkeys pulled fully laden carts while they were beaten relentlessly. When they passed and dropped something, nobody was particularly bothered. The poverty of the people and the district was blatantly obvious.

Some merchants looked as if they came from the country, and they sold what little of their home-grown vegetables they could afford to sell without starving themselves. Others attempted to flog something that they had gathered someplace else – such as worthless stones. Sleepy old men and women squatted at some corners and held out their hands, begging. Other people sat next to them, impassively. In some areas, especially near meat or fish shops, the smell of the leftovers that were scattered everywhere was disgusting. Filthy mop water was thrown out onto the street and the sandy ground turned into a mud pool, as only very few sections of the road had been cobbled. Scraggy feral cats roamed around looking for food in the refuse. This district gave us a feel for the concept of fighting for your life day after day. We felt that some people were even worse off than the roaming cats.

After a long search – we really thought that we were lost in a huge maze – we finally found our Riad Noga. We were more than happy to be back in our idyllic paradise.

Marianne freshened up and went to the roof terrace for some peace and quiet. I swam a few rounds in the pool, and then I perused the tour guides and brochures that were on display in the lounge. They outlined the history of the ancient imperial city of Marrakesh – formerly Mraksh, the name Morocco supposedly derived from that – and described all the ruling dynasties in great length. There was no way I could memorise all those exotic names. All that remained in my memory was the fact that the palm groves – the Palmeraie – had been cultivated almost a thousand years ago, and that one of the most famous and largest mosques of Morocco, the Mosque de Koutoubia, is in Marrakesh. It is situated on the western end of the Jemaa el-Fnaa.

I picked a restaurant for the evening from the leaflets. It was located in an old palace. When I tried to convince Marianne to accompany me there for dinner, she declined because she had befriended two Englishmen on the rooftop and wanted to have dinner with them in the hotel. I had asked the hotel to make a reservation for myself and asked one of the hotel employees to guide me, as I was worried I might get lost after our experiences previously this afternoon.

The restaurant was located in the eastern part of the medina near the city wall, about fifteen minutes walk from our hotel. The narrow roads and alleys were still as busy as they had been several hours ago. The city seemed to be in motion incessantly. Everywhere people were sweeping and cleaning, although that didn't make much sense as the dust returned instantly. Relying on my guide I took a good look around. Again, there were so many new and unfamiliar impressions! What amazed me the most was the way that almost archaic conditions coexisted as a matter of course with modern shops and technological achievements of modern times. Barely one hundred meters away from a derelict storage shed stuffed with rags, black wool, withered wood and charcoal, I saw large shops with the latest models of digital cameras and mobile phones. I stared gaping at all these overwhelming contrasts. My guide knew his way around Marrakesh but apparently, he didn't know the restaurant, so he had to ask twice before we found our way there.

Dusk was falling when we arrived at the restaurant. At first I didn't recognise it because the entrance was an inconspicuous door in a long, high wall that hadn't been painted in the antique pink, which is so typical for Marrakesh, but in a light beige. Above the door a small lantern shone a light on a small brass plate with the name of the Palais. We knocked with the metal doorknocker, and someone soon opened the door. I was led through an atmospherically illuminated corridor into a reception area with large wooden chests and opulent floral arrangements. When I entered the room I was greeted by a fragrant mist, as if a perfume with vanilla and nutmeg was being sprayed here. Someone led me into a courtyard with a glass roof where dining tables decorated with flowers had been arranged. Several open lounges surrounded the courtyard. While I was showed to my table we walked past a table with three guests. Suddenly a woman stopped and greeted me. It was the lady whose acquaintance I had made this morning in the café on the Jemaa el-Fnaa. Realising that I was on my own, she invited me to her table. I was happy to accept that invitation.

The other guests were an elderly couple from France who had owned a business in Marrakesh for several years. The husband came from a family that had been living in Marrakesh during the French protectorate. After Morocco had gained its independence he had returned to France with his parents. Later, however, he and his French wife had been drawn back to Morocco, and they had finally settled in Marrakesh. This was the perfect opportunity for me to find out more about the city and the people than the travellers guides had to offer.

As we were a group of four guests, we were offered a large, oven-baked fish as speciality of the day. The preparation would take a while but we enjoyed a delicious plate with starters and time went by pretty fast. The starters consisted of meat balls, meat skewers, olives, braised and pickled peppers and avocado quarters. Everything was exquisitely fresh and melted on our tongues.

I questioned my French conversation partner while we were waiting for the main course about the time of the struggle for independence as I hadn't found much about it in the travel guides. The man told me that the early stages of the national Moroccan independence movement had formed during the '30s of the 20th century. After the Second World War the population's demands for independency from the French and Spanish protectorate, that had been in place since 1912, had become increasingly stronger. When those demands were supported by Sultan Mohammed Jusuf in 1947, the French unseated him in 1953 and deported him to Madagascar. That prompted the entire population to support the Sultan, and for three years the political resistance increased, resulting in assassinations in Casablanca as well as cries for help to international organizations. In 1955 the French had to concede and call the deported Sultan back to a dire political emergency situation. The Sultan returned to Morocco triumphantly; the independence movement had been victorious.

In 1956 Spain and France officially recognised the independent state of Morocco, a constitution was elaborated and constitutional bodies were elected. In the wake of these events, many Europeans were evicted, or they left of their own accord because they were unsettled.

"Back in the Fifties, Morocco had a population of only about ten million; now there are 38 million, and that poses all the usual problems associated with such a population expansion", the French lady added. They told me that immigration had been re-opened several years ago. French people and other Europeans took residence in Morocco, founded companies and traded. International movie studios had settled around the High Atlas as the beautiful landscape offered a breathtaking backdrop for fantastic external shots. In fact, Marrakesh had turned into a Mecca for the international jet set of fashion designers, artists and hippies during the 1970s and 1980s.

After these highlights of Moroccan history, our main course arrived. The gratinated fish had been prepared in a large, oval clay dish, and it smelled delicious. It rested on a bed of tomatoes, peppers, carrots and potatoes and it had been garnished with herbs, olives and pieces of lemon. The white fish meat was firm but easily boned. The combination of fish and aromatic vegetables was an incredible indulgence. We drank an exquisite Sauvignon Blanc from Morocco. My companions told me that Moroccan wine is of good quality, and that it had become increasingly popular, despite having only a small market nationally, as the locals in the Orient and Morocco weren't allowed to drink wine. They told me much about their life in Morocco, their travels to the Atlas and the legendary hospitality of Moroccans. Unfortunately, I came to realise that I wouldn't have enough time for a journey to the Atlas during my few days here in Marrakesh to become acquainted with Moroccan families.

During our conversation and meal I had the opportunity to look around in the restaurant. It had been decorated with popular handicrafts, which we had already seen in the Musée de Marrakesh. Broad benches with large cushions stood along the walls in the side rooms, with low tables in front of them. Towards the open courtyard I saw upholstered furniture. The cushions and table cloths had been colourfully embroidered. The ceilings had been painted with bright ornaments, and the arches which served as doorways featured ornate stucco. Chiselled metal lanterns emitted subtle and mysterious light. The plates, bowls and dishes were covered in a dark green glazing, which complemented the ambience of the restaurant nicely. Andrè and Simone, my French companions, mentioned that this crockery came from a place near the Algerian border close to the city of Zagora in the south of Morocco. People in that area specialized in this kind of pottery.

Only a handful of guests were in the restaurant when we began our meal, but later it filled up considerably. Groups sat in the side rooms, drank tea, or ate their meals from the low tables. Large couscous bowls and huge tajines stood in the centre of the tables, and meat and vegetables were picked up from the shared dish with bread or fingers.

Our dessert consisted of a juicy, refreshing fruit salad made from pomegranate, oranges and pineapples.

Unbelievably it was now 11pm, but we had enjoyed our conversation and my new friends suggested visiting the bar of the "Les Jardins de la Koutoubia" hotel for a drink. They wanted to show me that modern house as a contrast to this rather traditionally styled restaurant, and they enthused about Marrakesh offering enough room for both tradition and the modern age.

We walked through the nocturnal medina to the bar. The hotel is located between the Koutoubia mosque and the Jemaa el-Fnaa, but we didn't choose to cross the square as we wanted to avoid the hustle and bustle there. Despite the late hour many people were still out and about.

The entrance to the hotel was in a small side alley. We entered through large glass doors and descended three steps to the hotel lobby. It opened out onto a spacious patio, and more glass doors were on the far side. Both areas had been panelled with dark to medium brown colours, and the floors consisted of beige marble. Brown leather furniture sank into deep-pile red carpets. Cleverly placed spotlights used the red carpets to create an inspirational atmosphere. The entrance to the bar was to the left of the lobby. The walls, the furniture and the glass door frames were also kept in all sorts of brown shades. The glass doors were hung with red, flowing curtains, and red lamps created a comfortable atmosphere. The bar and seating cushions were also red.

We sat down near the inner courtyard where we could see a swimming pool and a resting lawn with deck chairs and wicker furniture. Several other guests also enjoyed the cool night air by the bar. We ordered cocktails, talked quietly and listened to a pianist playing jazz songs in an unobtrusive volume. We spent probably about an hour and a half in this bar to end this wonderful evening in a very comfortable, pleasant atmosphere. A slight breeze wafted in occasionally, and I didn't want the evening to end.

As it had gotten fairly late we all ordered a taxi. I had to be driven around most of the historic town centre on the outside of the city wall as there was no way to cross the medina by car. In some areas the city wall was mysteriously illuminated. Leaving the taxi at the entrance to the alley leading to the Riad Noga, I tried to make my way past these high, bare walls as quickly as possible. The night porter in the guest house must have been waiting for my return as I was the last guest to come home, because he opened the door just as soon as I rang the bell.

Marianne was already asleep, and I carefully crawled into bed. It took a while before I fell asleep as I was all churned up inside from this wonderful evening, especially all the colours. I could still see all those mosaics and ornaments we had seen in our sightseeing tour during the day; I saw the warm green of the crockery in the restaurant, and most of all I saw the bright red of the carpets, curtains and lamps in the bar of the Les Jardins de la Koutoubia. Never before had I been inspired by colours in this way. I could feel the red in my body. It washed through every vein and cell. At the same time I could feel the green like velvet on my skin. This filled me with a revitalising tension and passion, while at the same time I felt an unbelievable tranquillity and peace. With magical and mystical feelings I fell asleep.

Our second day in Marrakesh began with yet another extensive breakfast on the rooftop. We took our time, planning our day. Among the leaflets, we had found an advertisement for a so-called "Hop-on/Hop-off Bus". If we used it we could take two tours visiting 25 landmarks of the city, and we were allowed to get on and off as many times as we wanted within 24 hours. The closest stop for this sightseeing tour was on the western end of the Jemaa el-Fnaa, so we crossed the square yet again. Near a small park carriage drivers dozed next to their respective transport in the shadows of the trees. We could have taken a sightseeing tour in one of those carriages but we stuck to our plan to use the bus. Sitting on the top floor of the open top bus we listened to the explanations that were provided in five languages.

Some of the tourist attractions visited during our bus tour were located on the outskirts of the medina, such as the Koutoubia mosque, Palais El Badi, Palais Bahia, the Saadian Tombs – a dynasty that had reigned in Morocco during the 16th century – the vast palm gardens and the Menara. We also passed through modern parts of the city, drove down the Avenue Mohamed V., which was lined with lush floral beds and orange trees, and crossed the Place de la Liberté. We learned that Marrakesh had been called the "Pearl of Southern Morocco" or "Red City" because of its red clay walls.

We also drove past the large and well-guarded Royal Palace, which the king only uses for special occasions these days, although he used to live here with his family and his entourage until recently when his new palace was built. The Royal Palace is set in a vast garden, and some of its tall palm trees were even higher than its outer walls. We heard that this garden had been open to the public for decades. The young king carried on this tradition because he wanted to give people the opportunity to relax in his garden, and he also wished to be in touch with his people. We were impressed about the positive attitude towards the king. We sensed from the words that he enjoyed the support and appreciation of his people, not just by virtue of his office but because he had an open ear for their concerns. Right next to the Royal Palace is the Kasbah, and yet another derelict part of the historic town centre with decrepit houses that were built even closer to each other than the ones we had already seen. And yet, there were still people living in them.

We completed both tours and decided to repeat them, in order to get off the bus at some of the landmarks. We learned a lot about Marrakesh and were greeted with many new impressions. While passing through the more modern districts of Gueliz and Hivernage we caught a glimpse of the modern way of life in Marrakesh, as opposed to the more medieval conditions in the medina.

Well administered first-class hotels, all the latest fashion design labels, leading makers of cars and many large companies were represented in Marrakesh, and evidently, business was good. On the outskirts of the vast Palmerai were city districts harbouring the villas of Marrakesh's rich inhabitants. Access to these areas was restricted, and they were enclosed by fences and walls. We saw noble hotels and holiday clubs, and even a lake with an exclusive beach had been built here. All this in a desert city!

While we sat drinking tea on the terrace of a small salon on the previous day, we had almost forgotten that we were in the 20th century; now, we sat on a boulevard in Gueliz, and looking around, we might as well have been in Rome or Paris.

When we returned to the hotel from our tour we were tired and weary, yet extremely impressed by the natural coexistence of noblesse and wealth on the one hand, and the poverty and decay that we had witnessed in several city districts and areas of Marrakesh on the other hand. There were people fighting for their livelihood on a daily basis, yet at the same time, there were people with money and wealth in abundance. Never before had I encountered such an extreme contrast, or was it just that I had not been susceptible to those kinds of impressions?

I relaxed on a suite in a quiet corner on one of the Riad's sheltered balconies. Here I found more books and magazines about Morocco. The parrot's crowing and chattering rang through the yard. It was fascinating listening to it because it recited words and short sentences it had learned throughout its time in the hotel. Then it sang different melodies and it seemed as if it was talking to itself. When it finally fell silent, I heard a quiet yet beautiful sound, something like 'wilkil, wilkil, wilkil'. It had to be a small bird somewhere in the courtyard's trees. I later discovered that it had been a bulbul. Listening to all these sounds in the silence of the Riad was charming and inspiring at the same time. The noises that were outside the house, and the barren walls of the medina had all but vanished from my thoughts. More than ever before, I felt as if I was in an oasis of harmony.

I became engrossed in an old book called "Marokko krizem krazem" (Crisscross in Morocco). It was a German text, written in Prague in 1962 by Jan Korinek. He wrote about his experiences in Morocco, starting in the 1920s until the 1950s of the 20th century. He must have written that book shortly after Morocco's declaration of independence. His recollection of the king at that time – who had been the grandfather of today's king – and his efforts to establish education, alphabetisation and industrialisation was astounding. Many of his impressions were similar to those we had encountered today, although fifty years had passed. Was it possible that during these decades nothing much had changed at all? Or was it tedious and difficult to enforce these changes?

The book gave great insight into the life of Morocco and I was certain that I would walk through Marrakesh with my eyes wide open from now on.

In a chapter about the Jemaa el-Fnaa he described the superstition, witchcraft and black magic that provided the basis for the market stalls of charlatans and quacks. They offered various herbs with natural healing powers – which have returned to the limelight with good reason – such as anise, basil, thyme, sesame, caraway, henna, sandarac, vinegar and many more that grew readily in the Atlas or even in the desert, but allegedly, certain markets also offered many obscure and strange remedies.

He wrote that according to superstition, many diseases were invoked by evil spirits called djinn. Therefore, a drop of oil that had been rubbed onto the verdigris of an old coin with a date was dripped into the mouth of newborn babies, so they would vomit and be free of evil spirits. Other rites were used in order to protect people from these spirits, or drive them away if someone had been possessed by one.

He had apparently learned a lot about the methods of these charlatans and witches by talking to the people. Amongst other things he described that an extract made from dead chicken or horse dung was a recommendation against mumps by these apothecaries of magic. Snails were being used against hair loss with young children. A woman who had been beaten by her husband was given the advice to roast hyena bristles, pulverise them and put them into his coffee to calm him down. Living or dried chameleons in oil, cooked with lavender, caraway, poppy and various other ingredients supposedly made for a potent healing potion, fighting various diseases. A scorpion caught on a Thursday and ground into a finer power served as a remedy for piles. Dried blood and fat from kidneys, taken from a sheep that had been slaughtered on the most important holiday Eid-el-Kebir, mixed with hair from dead donkeys and water from melted mountain snow was used to treat various wounds. Heads cut from living snakes were wrapped in reeds and then fastened onto children's clothing to protect them from spring diseases.

Of course, there were also numerous beauty treatments, regardless of whether they helped or not. Some also derived from superstition. Many women drew a black line around their eyes to protect themselves from evil. For a smooth and soft skin, the entails of a porcupine were mixed with the liver of a goat's stillborn kid. All these examples taken from the book were sufficient to open my eyes to all the oddities that were sold at the market stalls. Again, nothing much seemed to have changed during the past decades.

That evening, Marianne and I sat with the Englishmen in the Riad Noga. Just like on our first night we were about to start our dinner when the muezzins began their prayers, and their chanting reached our ears from all sides. The food was once again delicious. The cook had created a tasty salad from tomatoes, blue cheese and herbs. Our main course consisted of king prawns and rice with a lovely cream sauce, and mousse au chocolate was for dessert.

During dinner I told the others about what I had read and how Korinek described the Jemaa el-Fnaa and all that happened there. Our prominent place on the rooftop enabled us to see lights and smoke from the square. That motivated us to leave for the square at 11 pm. Marianne and her new friends had become curious by my narration.

Our curiosity was well rewarded. At night the square completely transformed. During the day it was filled with colourful hustle and bustle. In the darkness it turned into an unimaginable, almost magically circling of masses. We immersed ourselves in the crowd and just drifted along. Since the square is irregularly shaped we were only able to see small fractions of most areas, and we were permanently exposed to new insights and visions.

We soon recognised the carts with the oranges piled up on their loading area. Now they were set against the evening sky they seemed to be glowing even more. The merchants offered the freshly squeezed juice with even more enthusiasm than during the day. Next to these carts were stalls with melons, more fruits, nuts, pistachios, dates, figs and numerous other sweets. Light tarpaulin sheltered them, and lamps illuminated everything. Braids made from dried figs and nuts had been arranged in inviting patterns, creating temptation to steal them. Although we had eaten a full dinner, we couldn't resist nibbling here and there.

Right in the centre of the Jemaa el-Fnaa was a large area with big barbeques and cook shops. Long rows of tables and benches had been arranged around them. The tables had been laid with white plastic sheets. Skewers with meat, half or sometimes even whole lambs, mutton, poultry, offal, pieces of meat and steaks were being barbequed. The guests could watch their meat being carved, spiced and cooked above the embers. Skewers with meat and crispy fried mutton heads had been laid out to decorate the counters. Light bulbs hung above the benches. Thick smoke wafted from the barbeques because fat permanently dripped onto the glowing charcoal. We smelled herbs and meat. The people working there must have felt like being in a smoke box. The smoke wafted across the entire square, and it dawned on us then that this was what we had seen from the rooftop.

All tables were full. People ate and enjoyed the crispy pieces of meat, dipping them into a red sauce. Their side salad consisted of tomatoes, cucumber, onion and flatbread. We were replete; else we might have been tempted by the delicious smell to eat something, although we had been warned not to consume anything in open kitchens.

A variety of people were out and about on the square. Many tourists curiously strolled about, but many locals also wandered around. Dressed up young people, large families, women with babies cradled in their arms, old women with headscarves who linked arms with their daughters, young men in groups and loving couples were everywhere.

The cooks from the cook shops repeatedly tried tempting us with their foods. A beggar sat at one of the stalls, pushing a small bowl with bread aside to hide it – someone must have given it to him secretly. When he thought that he wasn't being watched he tried to steal a few pieces of meat from a fried mutton head, as he couldn't afford to buy the meat. Everyone chatted and laughed. The atmosphere on the square was very relaxed and full of the joys of life.

We were being moved around the square as if we had become trapped in a large stream. It seemed to me as if we circled around the various areas in a certain pattern and in spiral movements. Oriental sounds from the numerous musicians were everywhere. Sometimes the music was loud, sometimes more quiet – sometimes fast, sometimes slow. The characteristic Arabic melodies washed over us like rhythmical waves.

Even at this late hour, a multitude of merchants offered their wares next to the fruit stalls and cook shops. They had spread out their goods on the ground, and carbide or gas lamps tried their best to illuminate them. It felt eerie. Other than all sorts of oddities, mothballs, toys, cosmetic products and perfumes, the items that had been described in the book about Morocco such as herbs, salves, dried lizards, chameleons, ostrich eggs, seahorses, bird skulls, claws, roots, amulets, and vials with remedies were also on offer. All these magical mysteries were also purchased by people who didn't really look the superstitious type to me.

We watched a merchant reading a table beset with various symbols. Apparently, he was preparing a salve for a customer from fat and various powders according to his symbolic instructions. There were some stalls where women adorned young girls' or even older women's hands and feet with elaborate henna motives. Scribes sat on tiny stools, writing letters for people. The customers told the scribe what they wanted to send, and then they composed the letter. We watched unobtrusively, and were amazed at the earnestness of this procedure, which took place among this entire hubbub.

We had given any fortune-tellers and snake charmers a wide berth during the day, but the nightly fairytale atmosphere on the Jemaa el-Fnaa drew us in completely. A dancing group in white cotton garments wearing tall black hats and seashell necklaces danced amidst all the spectators. A young man explained to us that the musicians and dancers were members of an order that was renowned for spiritual dancing.

In another spot several men waited with little monkeys chained to their arms, looking for tourists who wanted a photograph with the monkey. Fire-breathers tried to attract attention, and cigarette merchants with bulky hawker's trays squeezed past while advertising their goods loudly. We heard the alternating sounds of tambourines, drums, violins and flutes. The music and the movement of the crowd increased and decreased like waves. Each one of the actors and jugglers fought with their means to draw people from the crowd and make them stand still, as that was the only chance they had to attract spectators.

We had stopped by a small group of acrobats. Six young Moroccans in red and blue pantaloons wearing white shirts executed daredevil stunts. They did cartwheels at unbelievable speed: side by side, towards each other and passing each other. They stood on their heads, somersaulted backwards to land on their feet again, and all that was performed in a breathtaking motion and in various formations. Two of them somersaulted upwards and landed on the shoulders of three other acrobats. They stretched out their arms, and using a rope they formed a triangle. Watching them was incredible, especially taking into consideration that they had no nets or mats or any other form of safety. They performed on the hard concrete floor. Their performance finished with some entertaining rope tricks and juggling with balls. The spectators gave a thunderous applause, and everyone gladly paid for this awesome performance.

In another area we spotted magicians performing their tricks. We felt as if we were visiting a large funfair – minus the immense technical extravaganza that was so common in Europe and the Western World. Instead, there were just people creating all the attractions with their body control, gestures and appearances, and they succeeded in providing thrilling entertainment for their audiences. They were well rewarded for it.

While we circled the square adrift in the waves of movement we found so many new, exciting and interesting things to focus on that we didn't realise how quickly time passed.

Close to the "Club Med" we saw a large crowd assembled in a semi-circle around three men. These wore djellabas and turbans and judged by their gestures, they were telling a story. We joined the crowd although we didn't understand a word as they were speaking Arabic or some kind of Berber language, but their passionate gestures during their performance captured our imagination. Now and then someone collected money from the audience, and we gave willingly as merely watching was interesting and thrilling enough. Shortly after the collection, a young man joined us and offered to translate the presentation into English for us. We accepted his offer, and paid him gladly for his service.

The story was about two brothers who had accompanied caravans from Timbuktu to Marrakesh many, many years ago. A caravan took three months to make this journey, transporting salt, gold, ivory and slaves. The former slave market at the Rahba Kedime – which is close to the Jemaa el-Fnaa – was still testament to these times, we were told. All the wares that were being sold in the souks of Marrakesh were transported back and forth for the merchants. The men described the legendary wealth of both cities in great detail. They also painted a grim picture of the exertions of working in a caravan. Twelve hours a day marching in the scorching heat were commonplace. At night, the desert always cools down considerably, and since they weren't allowed to bring much more than the transported goods, drinking water and just enough food to survive, all they could do against the cold was to wrap their djellabas and long blue headscarves around them, and lay close to the camels for warmth. Those three months across the desert and the Atlas Mountains were dangerous, as many footpads were after the goods and would ambush the caravans, killing the caravan escorts. Diseases and injuries could prove life-threatening during the long journey, as they had to be treated with what little medicine they had available.

The biggest obstacle, though, were sandstorms. In such conditions the caravan would be unable to proceed for days, and they didn't find any shelter in the vast desert. The fine sand would penetrate everything. Every time when they completed a journey, they were emaciated and dehydrated, seeking the small pleasures of city life in the trade centres. The two brothers were only ever able to spend a few weeks every year with their families in their home village in the Jebel Bani while they were eagerly awaiting the next caravan to assemble.

In the twelfth year of their career as caravan escorts they set off from Timbuktu. During the fourth week of their journey they experienced a sandstorm of epic proportions and feared that the world was coming to an end. The storm was so dense that the caravan got separated. For days they lay in the sand, hoping that the storm would die down.

Once the wind subsided, the older brother got up next to his companions, brushing off sand from his clothes and his face, and realising that his younger brother was gone. He had either fallen behind with the rest of the caravan, or he had taken another path. They searched the area but about a third of the caravan had vanished without a trace. As they needed water, and the sun had already begun burning down from the sky, they didn't have enough time for an extensive search. They couldn't delay any longer, and the caravan had to proceed if they didn't want to endanger their lives even further. All the way to Marrakesh the older brother tried to find out the whereabouts of his brother, and questioned every nomad they met. He also asked around in oases, whether anybody had seen or heard anything about the missing caravan members. But his brother and everyone else seemed to have vanished off the face of the Earth. When they finally arrived in Marrakesh, he couldn't enjoy the city life, as all he could do was search for his brother. He had no idea how he was supposed tell his parents about the loss, as they had entrusted him with his brother, asking him to look after him. In the end he had no other choice but to go home to his parents, bringing them the devastating news about the loss of their youngest son.

His parents prevented him from doing any more work for caravans after this tragedy, so he had to settle for growing dates in an oasis. He lived there miserably for several years under poor conditions, and he could not get over the loss of this brother. One day, he decided to go west along the Draa Valley to a city by the ocean as he had been told that working in the harbour paid well.

One day, he sat in a tearoom after he had finished his work as a day labourer in the harbour of Essaouira. Suddenly, he saw a middle-aged man who looked somewhat familiar. He followed him to a large house near the harbour. The entire demeanour and appearance of the man struck a chord within him, so he plucked up all his courage and knocked on the front door. Once he had been admitted, he asked for the man who had just entered the house. When the man approached him and asked what the matter was, he suddenly recognised his brother's voice, bolted towards him and embraced him. His brother, however, took a while longer to realise what was happening.

After many questions and a long conversation it became clear what happened after the stand storm. The youngest brother and part of the caravan had been cut off, ending up way behind the others, and had been fighting for sheer survival for several days. When they were almost starved and close to dying from thirst, nomads had picked them up and nursed them back to health. The recovery took a very long time, and in the end, the younger brother didn't remember where he came from and who he belonged to. Finally, he had joined merchants in a small town in the desert. He had journeyed to many places in remote areas before reaching this harbour city, where he had got taken employment with the harbour master, and later married his daughter. Once the two brothers had been reunited, they were both overjoyed. They brought their old parents the fantastic news, resettled them in the city, and the entire family lived there happily from then on.

The three storytellers emphatically performed this story with passionate gestures. The words in Arabic must have been flowery and full of emotion as even the translation was rousing. The young Moroccan spoke decent English but his vocabulary was obviously not as extensive as that of the actual storytellers. The audience had been listening intently; some were sitting on small benches they had brought with them. Watching these storytellers was captivating. They had to create the tension solely by narrative means, their gestures, and their facial expressions because they were not in a theatre and had no props or costumes. Despite the fact that the translation had turned it into a second-hand experience, we and the other tourists had been listening just as intently as everyone else, and we clapped our hands just as enthusiastically at the happy ending. Afterwards, we paused briefly, and then continued our relaxed stroll. It felt as if we had been listening to a fairytale from Arabian Nights.

Looking at the time while we walked along, we realised that it was already 1am. Many people were still on the Jemaa el-Fnaa, and the masses were still spurred on by the many attractions. All the cafés remained open. We decided to walk over to the central café with the rooftop terrace for another drink. We were lucky – a table right at the front of the top terrace had just been vacated before our arrival, so we had a fantastic view down onto the Jemaa el-Fnaa. We enjoyed another peppermint tea and took in the view.

Although it was well after midnight, the crowd didn't die down; on the contrary, it seemed as if the tension increased by the hour. Movement and music had intensified since our first rounds on the square and we felt that it was building up to a climax. Whatever that meant, we wanted to be there for it. We sipped our tea and talked about our experiences, but most of the time, we were busy watching all the encounters and the large crowd milling about on the square. Occasionally a horse and cart would appear on the edge of the square, dropping off passengers or picking up new ones. Mopeds and bicycles were squeezing through as always in the historic town centre; even some taxis dared to approach the square on occasion.

After 2am everything began to die down, without any notable reason or prior significant occurrence. Slowly, the place emptied, some booths were taken down and loaded onto small cars, and the market stalls around the square were being cleaned out and closed. Darkness also fell in the souks, and only a handful of people emerged from the alleys now. We paid for our beverages and made our way home.

When we walked across the Jemaa el-Fnaa towards the Rue des Banques – the liveliest way to our Riad – a young woman clad in a pink djellaba approached Marianne, speaking to her in French, English and German. She insisted we should accompany her to an old woman sitting next to a small table with an oil lamp. When we stopped, she explained to us in German and English that the old woman was a fortune-teller, and that she had pointed to us from a distance because she had seen that both women were facing many adversities. We declined resolutely but she didn't relent and finally, our companions opined that there was no harm in being a little yielding after an eventful evening such as this one. So we caved in and paid the negotiated price. The young woman explained that she would translate as the old woman only spoke a Berber dialect. We quickly realised that the young woman spoke fluent German and it was evident she had grown up there.

It was Marianne's turn first. She sat down on a small stool opposite the old woman, and the young woman sat next to her. Both our companions and I stood by. The old woman grabbed Marianne's hands, studied them from all sides, and then she took about ten small, round, smooth stones from a little pouch. Slowly, she dropped the stones through her fingers onto a small tray and began speaking quietly. The young woman translated just as soon as the older one paused.

First of all the fortune-teller spoke about the circumstances of Marianne's childhood and youth. I knew a lot about my best friend and noted that almost everything the old woman said was accurate. Gradually Marianne dropped her apprehensiveness, listening intently. After further statements about occurrences in recent years, the old woman said that Marianne had been deeply disappointed recently, and that she had not travelled to Marrakesh with the person she had intended to make the journey with initially. All that was correct, otherwise I wouldn't have been stood there at that particular moment. She added that this incident wasn't misfortune, but rather luck or even destiny, as she was now open for something new and magnificent. The old woman became all flustered, got up and hugged my friend, saying that Marianne was about to meet happiness like she had never experienced before in her life, and that all she needed to do was to embrace it. Again, she hugged Marianne tight and held her for a long time, gently stroking her cheeks. Finally, she abruptly sat down again on her stool.

What we had just witnessed left us perplexed, and we gave Marianne time to calm down and compose herself. Then, the old woman beckoned me over and gestured for me to sit down. She studied my hands from all sides as well. I felt her slender, soft and warm hands holding mine gently but firmly. I sensed a unique energy being emitted from those hands. When she let go of me, I felt a magnetic attraction to her and looked into her kind, gentle, wrinkled face beneath the large headscarf. She pulled smooth, round quartz stones of various different hues from her pouch, turning them in her hands and dropping them onto the small tray. I felt a tension rise within my body, while at the same time I felt inclined to trust her implicitly.

She began talking about my most recent past straight away and said that the strained life I had been living had stifled if not killed all emotions within me. She described me as a puppet on a string, with many people and powers pulling the strings in different directions. She claimed that I functioned according to the will of other people but not in line with my own opinions and beliefs. Even the person I was closest to was unable to drag me out, because he was experiencing much the same, if not worse. She added that we both had everything we needed for a good life, quite in contrast to the poor people on this square. While she talked to me sternly, she pinched my upper arm, warning me against continuing to live like that as I would miss out on life.

I wanted to object, arguing that everything was completely different, and that it was not our fault but instead that of circumstance. I thought about my agitation at the airport, about my suitcase where I had been everything but stifled or dead inside. But when I drew my breath to tell her about it, it was all too apparent that she wasn't interested in listening. She didn't intend to discuss issues with me at all. She continued, saying that my stay in Marrakesh was destiny, and that now I had the opportunity to free myself from the torpor. I merely had to walk through the city with my eyes, ears, nose and heart wide open. She also explained that I could absorb everything I needed from anywhere. I should discover my very own Marrakesh; that would be the key for a new life. Finally she emphasised that I shouldn't talk it to death. I also shouldn't attempt to change something instantly as circumstances would change if I allowed time to do some of the work for me.

She continued that I would soon have an epiphany, and that she had to prepare me for the time after that, which would consist of several difficult trials and tribulations. She predicted that I would despair many times because I would be alone for a long time, searching for a beloved person. But if I prevailed, believed in that person and passed more trials, I would finally understand life and the world as a whole. With those words she gently stroked my cheeks, looked at me affectionately and ended her monologue.

I was shaken, yet at the same time I was calm and collected. Marianne hugged me as if she wanted to comfort me. We said our goodbyes and returned to our guest house. Both our English companions had encouraged us to engage in this encounter but since they hardly spoke any German, they hadn't understood most of what the young woman had translated. Clearly they hadn't been bored though and had stood by watching the interaction with interest and compassion. Marianne and I were preoccupied while we walked back through the dark alleys, mulling over all we had heard. The two men were very considerate and didn't try to distract us or engage us in conversation. They admitted that everything had been very impressive for them. What they had witnessed had obviously had a deep impact, something they had not expected as they had thought fortunetelling to be the work of charlatans.

When we arrived back at the hotel it was 3am and all other guests were fast asleep. The night porter opened the door quietly after we rang, obviously awaiting for us to arrive back as he knew we were still out. He indicated their understanding for our late return, as it was fairly common for guests to arrive late when they visited the Jemaa el-Fnaa because it was a most interesting place during the night. I still felt wide awake and didn't want to bother Marianne with tossing and turning in bed. So I persuaded the night porter to give me access to the rooftop garden. He hesitated because that was not desirable during the night. Someone could quite easily climb onto the rooftop garden, and since that was dangerous, the door was locked at night. I finally managed to persuade him and fetched a blanket as it had turned quite cool. He had locked the door behind me and we had agreed that I would call his mobile phone if I wanted to return to my room. He would also come and see if all was in order during his usual rounds.

I cuddled up under my blanket and looked up to the sky. Since the city emitted lights from houses and lanterns, not too many stars were visible. I just pondered the day and all the experiences on the Jemaa el-Fnaa. I still didn't know what to make of everything that I had seen and heard. I had reached an emotional state where all sorts of thoughts assaulted me and whirled through my mind until I stopped thinking altogether. I drifted along in a space without thought or gravity in dark, quiet waters. After spending a long time in this condition I must have fallen asleep after all because I was awakened by the muezzins' voices. At first it was only one voice startling me. It increased in volume and gradually more voices added to it and enhanced it. Being all alone on the rooftop garden was a strange feeling. It was still dark, and I felt thrown into another world, another time, maybe even another person.

Long after the muezzins' chanting had ended, I still remained in that state.

When I thought about it the next day, I almost believed that I had opened a door to another reality.

I finally fell asleep again and woke up when the night porter came up to say goodbye as the employees of the dayshift had arrived. I returned to our room while the day began in the Riad. Marianne was still asleep and I also crawled under the blankets, falling into a restful sleep until about 11 o'clock.

Venturing into the New

As we appeared for breakfast late in the morning, it was being served for us in the inner courtyard. We ate baguettes, spaghetti dressed with argan oil and some cheese, and a large bowl with green salad. The lady of the house joined us and talked a while with Marianne and me. Our English friends had left for a tour of the surroundings of Marrakesh early in the morning. The lady of the house told us that argan oil was extracted from nuts, and that the vast, thorny argan trees grew exclusively in Morocco's southwest and in the High Atlas. The attempt to cultivate them in Israel and Algeria had failed miserably. The production process for argan oil was also very complex. Women had to process the nuts with their bare hands, as the nuts are extremely hard, and they can only be opened by knocking a certain spot of the shell hard onto stones. Therefore, this delicacy which was becoming increasingly popular with gourmet chefs all over the world was extremely expensive outside of Morocco; within its borders it was still reasonably priced. The oil is very aromatic, and evoked different flavours in different dishes. The slight taste of nuts enhanced the taste of lamb, while couscous brought out a taste of sesame. The most popular use, though, was for breakfast. The combination of flatbread dipped into argan oil, almonds and orange blossom honey was regarded as an absolute delicacy, because the sweet honey and the almonds harmonised with the oil's nutty aroma. It sounded mouth-watering, and we almost felt like starting over with our breakfast. The spaghetti was also incredibly tasty with a fine aroma of nuts that I had never tasted before.

We finished our extensive breakfast and lounged in the shadows of the inner courtyard, still shattered from the excitement and the long night on the Jemaa el-Fnaa. In fact, we didn't feel like any more distractions from downtown today. The lady of the house recommended we should indulge in a wellness session in a hamam. She said that there were many of them in the historic town centre, and that they were difficult to recognise as they usually resided behind inconspicuous doors and facades. A visit to a hamam is compulsory for the locals. Most houses in the historic town centre had poor sanitary facilities at best, and the people craved regular and thorough cleaning for religious reasons if nothing else. She recommended a more dignified, western-oriented hamam for our first visit to Morocco. Apparently, one had opened not far from the Riad about a year ago. It sounded promising, so we had asked her to book an appointment for us an hour later for an all-round-cleaning-massage-and-relaxation-session.

After our breakfast we browsed the small library and found a description of a hamam among the travel guides. We quickly found that the so-called hamams that had opened recently in some saunas at home had little to do with their cousins in Oriental countries. They appealed more to our western imagination and fantasies. The journalist Muriel Brunswig-Ibrahim described in her book that the hamam is both a steam bath and a news broadcasting centre at the same time, and that they are essential to daily life in Morocco. The women either had set days for their visits to hamams, or there were strictly separated areas for men and women. The bathhouses replaced the teahouses – here, secrets were disclosed and marriages sealed, wrote Brunswig-Ibrahim who had apparently travelled the length and breadth of Morocco, maintaining good relations with the people and getting to know their ways. When women and children occupied the bathhouses, the laughter, chatter and giggling was incredible. The hamam was popular for many reasons; one of them being that a body treatment removed all old layers of skin and redundant hair, while at the same time the customary timidity and reclusiveness of Moroccan women made way for free and unimpeded interaction. However, before leaving the hamam feeling all refreshed and gloriously clean after a few hours, one had to first submit to certain tortures.

Just before we wanted to set off for our visit to the hamam, the doorbell rang and someone handed me a small letter. I was perplexed – who would send me a personal note here? I read the letter and was pleasantly surprised to read that the French couple, André and Simone whom I had spent my second evening here in Marrakesh with, had invited me to a festivity at their friends' house in the district of Hivernage. They wrote that they would pick me up at 8pm in a taxi, and that I would surely enjoy it, as there were many lovely people to meet. I was touched and gladly accepted the invitation.

Marianne and I set off for the hamam, feeling very curious after what we had read. We just needed to turn three corners to reach the entrance of the plain house that was situated in a small alley. A plate with Spa written on had been mounted above the door. Again, you could not judge the inner qualities of the house by its outward appearance. We walked through a short, dark corridor on the ground floor and emerged into a bright, open courtyard. A rectangular, shallow metal basin with a broad, grey satin-like edge was embedded in the ground. Rose petals drifted in the water. Four large metal plant tubs with large green plants stood around the basin. All walls of the courtyard, the adjacent rooms and the upper levels had been painted in light grey lime paint. Dark brown, wooden tables and chairs of a plain design, as well as sofas with crème-white linen upholstery stood in an open alcove and in the adjacent rooms that could be entered through glass doors. Large mirrors in dark brown wooden frames hung on the walls. Everything had been kept in warm, unobtrusive hues, and music played quietly in the background. We were greeted by young employees in dark and crème coloured linen clothing, and they asked us to be seated in a quiet corner. We were offered thé, coffee and some biscuits. Several other visitors also sat in the courtyard and talked quietly, relaxing in their bathrobes between treatments or waiting to be fetched for their next treatment. Everything was calm and relaxed.

After about ten minutes an employee carrying an open bag made from bast containing a fluffy bathrobe appeared, leading us into a cabin where we could get changed. We were then collected, and our normal clothing was placed into the bast bag and placed into storage. We were lead up a narrow stairway to the second floor, where we were shown into different rooms. My room was low, dimly lit and humid, and the walls had been plastered with dark pink tadelakt. A couch with a plastic-looking cushion stood in the centre of the room, and a large basin with steaming, warm water was in one corner of the room. Another employee was already waiting for me. She asked me to take off my bathrobe and poured the contents of a small bowl with warm water over my shoulders and body, before asking me to lie down on the couch.

I had ordered a treatment with 'delices', with sweets. The sweets consisted of honey in oil with large sugar crystals. She took a handful of that liquid from a bowl and started rubbing down my entire body with it. She did that for about a quarter of an hour, and she applied quite a bit of pressure in the process. At first it hurt a little because the sugar crystals prickled and chafed but after a while I noticed that the effect was that of a strong peeling, and that the honey and oil gently soaked into my skin. I closed my eyes, felt the warmth in the room and the gentle rub on my body and indulged in the treatment. Once she finished, she asked me to get up and poured warm water over me again to wash off the remaining sugar crystals.

Someone else arrived shortly afterwards and led me back to the courtyard, where Marianne arrived virtually at the same time. We relaxed listening to the quiet music. Most visitors here were young people, some of them apparently tourists.

Several magazines in French were available, and I indulged in a thick fashion journal and an art magazine. That way I could get some insight into the modern Morocco, as the magazines pretty much dealt with the same subjects as those in Europe. They reported about fashion shows or exhibitions from globally renowned fashion designers, but they also portrayed up-and-coming Moroccan agencies or companies that had developed their very own interesting style. They announced cultural highlights and described upcoming events. Especially successful Moroccan business women were being interviewed, and their merits and achievements were introduced in great detail. I also found reports about the Royals and their international family relations – for example with the Bulgarian royal family. I hadn't even known that there was such a thing as a royal family in Bulgaria. So these magazines conveyed the modern Morocco to us here in this almost medieval historic town centre.

After a relaxation period of about three quarters of an hour we were again greeted, this time being led to some side rooms on the ground floor where we would receive our massages. Candles had been lit in the room, and the large glass door leading to the courtyard had been closed. Crème coloured curtains provided a dim, comfortable light. The oil that was being used for my massage smelled of roses and jasmine, and a hint of lavender also wafted through the air in the room. I made myself comfortable on the large towels that covered the couch and switched off my thoughts. Before the massage I was generously covered in oil. Since my skin was all soft and smooth from the previous treatment, the oil soaked into my skin straight away. The masseuse began with gentle movements from my torso outwards along my limbs. Then she began to knead all my muscles and parts of my body, ranging from very gentle to fairly rough grips. The treatment lasted for an hour and I really felt every single muscle in my body after that.

Our feel-good program also included washing our hair and a facial, which gave us time to recover from the invigorating-yet-exhausting massage. Three hours later we started back.

I had considered buying something to wear for my evening invitation because my suitcase still hadn't arrived, so we took the Rue Dabachi to the souks. I looked everywhere but couldn't find anything that I liked. Eventually, we crossed the Jemaa el-Fnaa to reach a cobbled shopping mile which was on the far side of the large square. We found a great variety of shops, and their atmosphere differed greatly from that in the souks. We even found shops with modern clothing. Although this area was busy, it wasn't quite so crowded. I finally found something in a shop with imported Indian clothing and bought a comfortable suit made from georgette in dark petrol blue with flared trousers. The top was made from one piece with a scoop neckline featuring a slit that made pulling it over your head much easier. It had long sleeves, and extended down to my thighs. All seams had been adorned with a large, embroidered border in yellow and gold. The combination with the petrol blue was beautiful. I also bought a bright yellow silk scarf.

Satisfied, we walked back across the Jemaa el-Fnaa. Suddenly we met Jack and Ted, our English friends from the hotel, as they had just returned from their day trip. We were happy to see them, exchanging stories about our day as we continued our way together.

We stopped frequently because we had all become fascinated by the Jemaa el-Fnaa after the amazing events of the previous night. We saw a crowd of people gathering around some snake charmers. At first there was nothing special to see. Four men in the centre of the group wearing caftans and turbans had baskets next to them, presumably with snakes inside. Then one of the men carefully reached into the basket, pulling out long, grey snakes that hardly moved. He removed rattle snakes from another basket and put them down on a cloth. One of the four men started playing the flute, while another played a small drum. When they noticed us and several other tourists, they demanded payment for the performance. We were reluctant at first, but then we agreed to pay a few Dirhams and continued to watch. The flute, the drumming and the erratic movements of the snake charmer unsettled the snakes. They slowly bobbed up, and it seemed as if the upper part of their body was dancing. The snake charmer picked up one snake, wrapping it around his legs and one hand. Another, apparently a local spectator, told us in French that this would dispel ailments from limbs. Another spectator approached the snake charmers and gave them some money. Our translator explained that he wanted to be cured from an affliction in his arms, and that he wanted the snakes to banish the evil spirits. So the snake charmer twirled the snakes around this man, wrapping them around his arms. The melody of flute and drums increased in volume and tempo. The snakes writhed, the sick man moved erratically, threw his arms up into the air, rolled his eyes – and suddenly stopped. The snake charmer took the snakes away from him and put them back in their basket. The man with the snake treatment convulsed, stroked with his palm down his arms and finally embraced the snake charmer full of gratitude. The crowd applauded and our translator told us that the man apparently felt healed, since he didn't have any more pain in his arms. We remained there for a while, talking amongst ourselves. One of the Englishmen, Jack, told us that he had seen even more magnificent tricks from a snake charmer in Agadir during another of his visits to Morocco. The man had teased the snake, whipped it around his face in ecstasy and finally, he had tried to swallow it. We were all convinced that this had been nothing more than a little theatrical performance, but it had been compelling, and we had to admit it was interesting entertainment and it had magically enthralled us despite our knowledge of the facts of life. That said, we were not entirely sure that this didn't qualify as cruelty against animals.

At 8pm sharp my friends rang the door bell at the Riad and picked me up by taxi. We left the historic town centre through the next gate and drove off in a south-westerly direction until we arrived at the Boulevard El Yarmouk in the district of Hivernage. My friends told me in the taxi that several of their friends hosted festivities around this time of year, and that one of them was taking place tonight. Usually, these events were attended by both business people from various nations living here in Marrakesh as well as many Moroccans. It was customary not to discuss politics or business on these nights, and asking about professions or where people came from was also frowned upon. The idea was to gather, engage in light conversation and talk about literature, music and culture. I had donned my new outfit and felt very comfortable in the light material with the beautiful colours. I was wondering what was awaiting me.

It was still light when we arrived, stopping outside a large villa with a magnificent garden. We were warmly welcomed, and just as my friends had told me, nobody asked where I came from or what I was doing in Marrakesh. My friends were my ticket for entry. First we passed through a large reception room, and then we crossed a spacious salon into the back garden. Several groups of people had gathered, chatting amicably. When we passed the third group, I recognised the lady from the Jemaa el-Fnaa who had introduced me to my new friends. She was obviously pleased to see me and whispered, "I have been expecting you. I'm sure you will enjoy this evening". She asked us to join her, and we were offered an aperitif. Small starters had been arranged on several tables near the house, and everyone helped themselves to the pleasant refreshments. The predominant languages were English and French, and occasionally I heard some Arabic. It was pretty apparent, though, that most guests didn't understand it, and most Moroccans spoke fluent French and passable English anyway. The conversations focused on art, movies, the annual movie festival, and exhibitions in Marrakesh. Some talked about classical music and the most recent pop concert that had taken place in the El Badi Palace. Although subjects of the entire international art scene were included in the conversations, sooner or later Marrakesh would be the topic again. It felt as if Marrakesh was the primary theme of this evening.

When darkness fell, lanterns were being placed in the garden. The villa was illuminated by halogen lights and glowed in light pink. I went into the house with my female friend who had accompanied me all evening and had introduced me to many people. We wandered through several rooms that had been decorated in a modern and subtle style. Large rose bouquets had been arranged in the salon as decorations, while white amaryllis served as eye catchers in the reception area. Every room was illuminated in a different colour with halogen lights. One room featured a light blue, another yellow, yet another green and so forth. What's more, different fragrances had perfumed the various rooms, and we smelled vanilla and cinnamon, the purple room smelled of lavender, the blue one of violets, the red salon smelled of roses and so forth. We heard subtle music everywhere from classical through to blues, jazz, swing, pop and Arabian music. Thus, a different atmosphere had been created in each room which could be perceived with all senses.

We meandered from room to room, engaging in small talk with other guests. One group discussed the new plants in the Jardin Majorelle, which was not far from the villa in the district of Gueliz, and the stunning bloom had been even more enhanced. Picnics in the Palmerais were another topic. Apparently they were a huge annual event and attracted thousands of people from Marrakesh to the old palm tree orchards for festivities. When we were notified that dinner had been served next door, we walked over. In the middle of the massive kitchen stood a large wooden table set with many soup plates, dozens of spoons and several baskets filled with flatbread. On a large oven was a large cauldron containing a stew that smelled simply delicious. Even the illumination in this room was homely. Only strip lights on the upper cupboards and the extractor hood had been switched on to prevent glaring light disturbing the otherwise cosy atmosphere. I learned that this was a

Moroccan-style stew made from mutton, onions, dates, olives, figs, raisins and spiced with cinnamon and aniseed. The combination was both sweet and salty-spicy, depending which ingredient touched your tongue. All the guests helped themselves to flatbread and a ladle full of stew, and stood in the kitchen or the adjacent dining room eating. Some – including myself – came back for a second helping as it was absolutely divine.

After the stew, red wine was served. It should have been served during dinner; however, it would have been almost impossible to hold a plate, a spoon and a wine glass at the same time. The conversations continued, and some people started dancing in a large room. The mood became more cheerful. I don't remember when it started, but more and more guests gathered in the salon and began chatting about what Marrakesh meant to them. Some kind of a game developed from there, and several rows of guests formed a circle. One guest would step into the centre of the circle, singing about the merits of Marrakesh using always the same melody. Sometimes, it was just one word, sometimes whole sentences. I remember fragments such as: Marrakesh – oasis in the desert; Marrakesh – open gate to the desert; Marrakesh – city of poets; Marrakesh – red city; Marrakesh – city of the Seven Saints; Marrakesh – city of the Almoravids, Almohads and Saadi; Marrakesh – testament to Sultan Youssouf ben Tachfine; Marrakesh – city of tranquillity; Marrakesh – city of orange trees; Marrakesh – city of jacaranda trees; Marrakesh – city engulfed in scorching heat by the sirocco; Marrakesh – city of roses; Marrakesh – city of palm trees; Marrakesh – city with the famous Hotel Mammounia. After every sentence, the entire crowd joined in with the refrain: "Ma-, Marra-, Marrakesh", clapping their hands. This went on for quite a while, and the mood became increasingly rapt and exuberant. This game went on for a long time, as nobody had any inclination of stopping. Everyone seemed to be in some kind of trance, drawing the whole room of individuals together with the beguiling theme of Marrakesh, until everybody mysteriously, but oh-so-naturally arrived together at the crescendo: "Ma-, Marra-, Marrakesh". Eventually, as some participants began to tire, the chanting died down and flared up again here and there before it finally faded completely. Several people left the room quietly, while others remained in silence. It didn't seem appropriate to engage in idle conversation now. It was a magical moment, and everybody felt the same way.

André and Simone had arranged a signal if any of us wanted to go home. They had insisted on taking me back personally, and didn't want me to leave by myself in a taxi. I saw their subtle signal, said goodbye to my friend and headed for the exit. The taxi was waiting outside the fence, and we climbed in, still overwhelmed by our emotions. The villa was still beautifully illuminated, and I looked back wistfully.

As we left, I smelled the wonderful fragrance of a tree that only exudes its fragrance at night. Another one of those trees stood in the courtyard of our hotel and every time I returned late at night I would inhale and enjoy this splendid aroma. It still lingered inside the taxi. The driver went down the Avenue Mohammed V into the historic town centre, drove along the wider roads in the south of the medina that followed the inside of the city walls, and took many corners before finally stopping on the road where the alley to my hotel forked off. We hadn't spoken the entire time because all three of us were still moved by everything that happened during the past few hours. I told them that I had enlisted for the event that was taking place in the El Badi Palace on the next evening, and wanted to attend. I had talked to two Moroccan ladies during the evening, and they had told me about that event. We wanted to meet there the next evening. My friends accompanied me to the Riad and we bid each other a warm good night. I thanked them for the invitation as I would never have met that many nice people as a normal tourist. André and Simone were obviously pleased by my gratitude. The night porter had waited for me, as once again I was the last person to return home. He must have considered me to be a true night owl. This time, I quickly went to bed and fell asleep with the melody of"Ma-, Marra-, Marrakesh" still resounding through my mind. For the first time in a long time, I felt as if I belonged and always had done.

On the fourth morning I decided to go swimming, as the muezzins' morning prayers had wakened me before 5am and I wasn't able to get back to sleep. After spending the previous days and nights filled with an exhilaration of senses and experiences, I had started thinking long and hard in bed that morning. I recalled everything that had made an impact on me since I had arrived and asked myself, which one of all these events could be my personal secret, the charm that the fortune-teller had foreseen for me? I came to no conclusion. Although this city was a new, exotic, interesting and impressive little bubble, it still didn't give me that exceptionally special feeling that my mysterious friend had predicted. I had been impressed by the predictions of the old woman on the Jemaa el-Fnaa; now, however, I just cast them aside, laughed at myself from a rational point of view, and admonished myself not to waste any time thinking about such mumbo jumbo.

I enjoyed the swim. A current generator increased the effort required to cross the pool, and it felt as if the basin was longer than it looked. After an hour of intensive swimming I took a long shower and accompanied Marianne for breakfast on the rooftop garden. I wanted to break it to her gently that yet again, I had plans for the evening that didn't include her. But I found that I didn't have to feel guilty for spending most evenings of our holiday with other people, when she told me bashfully that she had fallen in love with Jack, one of the Englishmen. So she was quite relieved that I did my own thing during the evenings, and she could spend time with him. During the day, Jack and Ted usually played golf or took trips into the countryside, so we had plenty of opportunities to spend time together.

On this day we paid the districts of the tanners and dyers a visit. They were located in the eastern part of the medina, and once again we found ourselves walking along endless alleys. When we arrived we saw the familiar picture of many people pushing through alleys, small shops, crafts-man workshops, small mosques, and old, high loam houses that didn't have windows. Bicycles and mopeds were being repaired in one backyard; in another, we even saw cars being fixed – while cars in the historic town centre were a rarity they were still able to drive around the outskirts. Later we saw an increasing number of tourists and tour parties with their guides. Teenagers approached us frequently, offering to take us to the square – the Jemaa el-Fnaa – or into the tanner quarter. It was quite difficult to get got rid of them but we had no intention of ending up in some carpet shop where they would try to sell us overpriced goods and badger us indefinitely.

Once we reached the tanner quarter we realised why these places were so immensely attractive for tourists, and why the boys would look for gullible buyers here. Not everyone was as cautious as we were. What we saw was a scene that might have been set in ancient times.

In numerous large pits lined with bricks uncountable pieces of leather were being tanned under the open sky in a terribly stinking swill. This method of working was still the same as it had been hundreds of years ago, and until now we had only read about it in books about the Middle Ages, or in novels and documentaries. In the swill young men in dirty work clothes stomped about barefooted. Their legs and arms were covered with the whitish sludge as they trampled around pressing the animal hides into the tanning liquid. Other men stirred the pits with long poles. When they were done, they hung the tanned leather out in long rows around the outside of the area to dry. Afterwards it was processed in small huts, or it was stored in large piles. In between the bustle, gaunt dogs and cats roamed around. The workers were unperturbed by the tourists standing around – some holding their noses – and taking photographs. If a spectator came too close to the stone pits they would shoo them away.

We were unable to stay long as the pungent stench of the untanned hides that still had decaying pieces of meat attached to them was unbearable. We swiftly walked away, shivering at the thought that the tanners had to do their hard work here day in, day out. Working in the dyers quarters was also hard and probably even health-damaging but the scenery was much more appealing due to the bright colours. Large tubs had been placed next to each other, and wool, cloth and leather was being died in different liquids before being hung up to dry. The bright colours ranged from red through yellow and green to blue, with nearly all the hues in between. Young and old men worked here. Large amounts of undyed pieces were squeezed into the various tubs and pressed down with large poles or even bare hands. They had to be moved around so that they soaked in the colours. Several workers even stamped around in the tubs, and their work clothes and skin were covered with the colour. We had no idea how they would ever wash themselves clean again.

This area was also very busy, and many children ran around. The coloured textiles and wool were processed in houses and yards around the square. We saw huge balls of wool in many colours in one backyard, and people walked in and out of there. They were probably carpet manufacturers or merchants, wanting to inspect the wool to negotiate a good price. Some wool was loaded onto small transporters. Inside the houses we saw bales of cloth that had been piled up to the ceiling. We felt as if we were looking at a larger than life colour scale.

Women were busy measuring and cutting the fabrics inside some of the houses. We couldn't get enough of all these colours because this area was so vastly different from the consistently clay-coloured districts of the historic town centre.

After strolling around for a long time we headed towards our next destination, the city district of Gueliz and the Jardin Majorelle. In order to reach it we had to cross the medina diagonally in a western direction. Suddenly, we came upon a large building site. A high fence made of corrugated iron surrounded a large area that must have covered several blocks. Donkey carts transported construction waste off that area. Someone must have bought an entire district of the historic town centre. We discovered a sign that announced in Arabic and French that a 'Creative Centre' was being built here. Whatever that was supposed to be, we wondered if it was really suitable for the historic town centre.

We passed the Medersa and the mosque Ben Youssef, which we had seen during our first walk through town, before we walked through the city wall at the Bab Mousoufa. Truth be told, we were very glad to have arrived in an area with an European look. After the long walk through the throng in the historic town centre, the pushing and shoving of moped and bicycle drivers, the endless rows of donkey carts, the noise and the dust really unnerved us, and all we wanted was some peace and quiet.

Gueliz had been established during the French protectorate. Broad avenues lined with trees led through it. Here, we found modern shops, medical practices, law firms, company headquarters, restaurants, bistros, travel agents and hotels. The side roads led to residential areas with multi-storey houses boasting anything between five and eight floors. Many shops and small restaurants were located along these roads. We saw plenty of construction works, as some houses were being reconstructed; some were undergoing conversions, and others being newly built. Close to the stop for the sightseeing bus we found an appealing restaurant featuring a rooftop garden with large shelters. We slumped into wicker chairs and rested a while before having a little snack. While we were eating Marianne and I recalled all the things we had seen during the previous days, and I said to her: "As much as I envy our landlady of the Riad for living in such an exotic and impressive city with a wonderful, warm climate, I'm glad to be going home in a few days time. Today, the Oriental way of life is simply too much for me, and I don't think I could bear it in the long run". Marianne opined that I had some kind of holiday or Marrakesh blip, and that I would feel much better once we had a breather. She was right.

After an hour of relaxation beneath the shelters of the restaurant we headed towards the Jardin Majorelle, which was easily accessible on foot. Once there, we were torn between awe and delight. The Jardin Majorelle is a part of Yves Saint-Laurent's garden that is open to the public. He owned a large town house in Marrakesh. Small white pebble paths and paths with red bricks wound their way through the garden, some of them defined with blue walls. Tiny rivulets splashed in blue-painted stone pipes. We saw alleys lined with bougainvilleas, and pergolas covered with green climbing plants. Several small, blue fountains were scattered amongst the plants. Beautiful park benches had been placed in quiet spots in between the garden plants, or they stood next to rounded walls that had been painted in the customary dark pink of Morocco. A bright blue stone house was hidden behind bushes but we noticed it nonetheless because it was positively radiant.

The garden contained plants galore. Huge date trees rose up to the sky next to smaller phoenix palms. Flower beds full of grasses, bushes and colourful flowers caught our eyes. Ivy climbed up on trees and walls, trumpet flowers, hydrangea and climbing roses soaked up the sunlight that shone down through the canopies. We spotted uncountable plant pots, some yellow, some blue, others of more natural colour. Some of them were made of glazed ceramic, while others were plain clay. Magnificent geraniums or hibiscus added to the floral diversity. We could smell and distinguish orange and oleander trees, lavender, jasmine and even eucalyptus. In another spot we found a large flowerbed with sand where tiny cactuses had been planted. The trees were full of singing birds, while butterflies and dragonflies fluttered around. We couldn't get enough of this paradise and wandered around from one corner to the other. We found a little inscription that informed us that the painter Jacques Majorelle had cultivated this garden during the 1920s and that it harboured plants from all five continents. When he died, the garden became overgrown until Yves Saint-Laurent reconstructed and re-cultivated it. He was so pleased with the newly developed floral abundance that he decided to revert to Majorelle's initial practice by opening at least part of his garden to the public. Full of admiration for the beauty he had created here, we stole a glimpse of his house that stood behind the garden wall.

Our stay in the Jardin Majorelle had lifted our spirits after we had hit a bit of a plateau at lunchtime, and we decided to pay a well-known leather shop called "Birkenmeyer" a visit that was only a few roads away. It had been recommended to us because they sold reasonably priced leather goods 'Made in Morocco'. They also sold designer products, such as Burberry and other labels, for slightly lower prices if they had minor faults. The medium-sized shop was located in a side road of the Avenue Mohamed V. It was not very well illuminated and crammed full of goods. Since a large party of tourists had invaded the shop just before our arrival the sellers seemed somewhat nervous and a little abrupt.

We browsed the shop for a while and found three items that fitted and were fairly cheap in comparison to the prices at home.

After our little shopping trip, we headed for the bus stop because we had decided that this was a good time to give the city bus a try. On the way we got sidetracked by a small and exquisite shop with handmade chocolates. The chocolates had been decoratively spread out, and the friendly staff gave us a few taste samples to tempt us. We ended up buying a whole box of chocolates because they were so delicious. Further down the road we found a very modern and extremely clean butcher. Compared to the stalls in the souks and the medina – especially the open meat market at the southern end of the Jemaa el-Fnaa where animal halves hung out in the open – this shop appeared to be very inviting. This day had once again showed us the vastly different worlds of Marrakesh – the historic town centre where time has been standing still for centuries, and the new world that is second to none in terms of being modern and exclusive to any cultural centres in Europe.

We took the overcrowded city bus, left it at the Koutouba mosque and crossed the Jemaa el-Fnaa to reach our Riad since there was no faster way of getting back.

Since it had now become some kind of a habitual ritual, we drank thé à la menthe on the rooftop of the Café de France, enjoying the evening sun as if all of this had always been part of us.

When we arrived back at the Riad, I had to hurry because I had to wash off the dust, get changed and get ready for my date in the evening. Jack was waiting for Marianne and both of them disappeared quickly to the rooftop.

I had ordered a taxi for 8pm, which took me to the Badi Palais. This Palais is the ruin of a vast 16th century palace.

Most of the buildings have been destroyed and only the outer walls remain, although several rooms still exist in the southern and eastern parts. They are not accessible though. To the left of the entrance is a stairway that leads to the upper level of the derelict building where people can get an overview over the vastness of the site. The Place des Ferblantier is in front of the site, and a path leads to the entrance between the high clay walls. Many storks were nesting on the walls. That evening, the path was lined with torches, and many guests headed towards the gate. The whole atmosphere was somewhat magical, which was also owed to the storks and their nests, which protruded over the rim of the wall. When we had visited the palace in broad daylight all this had seemed a little morbid; but now, the walls oozed a completely different, mysterious atmosphere. My new Moroccan friends were awaiting me at the entrance.

I hardly recognised the interior of the palace. Large, burning candles had been placed in small niches along the entire outside wall. Their flickering flames made the dark beige walls appear in a different and warm light, literally. Inside the building about twenty large basins containing orange trees and water had been decoratively spruced up. Large burning torches had been placed around the outside and between the orange trees, and large glass bowls drifted on the water with burning oil lamps. Occasionally little water jets shot up, creating picturesque effects. When we had been here two days ago, the basins had only contained a little water, now they were full and deeply attractive. Along the outer walls, white canopies had been arranged on the stone floor. Standing beneath them were decorated tables beset with oil lamps. We were led to our table through this amazing atmosphere.

On the way there we met my friend from the Djemaa el-Fnaa again. She welcomed me and whispered that she had been waiting for me as always and that I should enjoy this evening.

Our baldachin offered enough room for about twenty people. Myself and the two Moroccans, whose names were Sfia and Fatima, sat on a table that had been laid for three. We had a good view of the area, and I realised that the rooms in the southern part, which used to be the chambers for the sultan's favourite wife in former times, were open on this evening. Apparently they were being used for catering. To the left was a small stage, where tonight's musical entertainment would be provided. The event had been announced as the "Lalla and Couscous Festival" with Oriental music by Moroccan artists and Gnawa music. Fatima explained that a popular Moroccan group would play first. They played pop music with Oriental elements and were one of the reasons why this event was so well-frequented. After dinner, a group of black Gnawa musicians would perform. According to legend, Gnawa musicians originated from Sudan. They had been on their way north, when they decided to remain in the beloved city Marrakesh. Apparently the irresistible and enchanting drums and songs of the Gnawa musicians usually made women dance uncontrollably. 'Lalla' in Moroccan means something like ladies, women, or princesses, and they are usually addressed with that term. When I looked around closely, I noticed that all the guests were female. That left me extremely curious.

First of all we received a cool, freshly squeezed orange juice and walked around for a while. My new friends stopped at several tables or small groups that had gathered between the tables in front of the stage and talked to other women. The mood was cheerful and relaxed, and everyone was joking and laughing. It was interesting for me, although I hardly understood anything when people talked in French. When we passed the catering area, I saw couscous being prepared in large pans. I could smell the enticing scents of saffron, cumin and other spices.

After a while of informal conversation someone addressed all the guests from the stage, asking them to return to their tables as dinner was going to be served. Shortly afterwards the music started playing. Many young women in bright, naturally coloured trouser suits swarmed out, carrying large, blue glazed ceramic bowls full of couscous to the tables. We were offered a choice of a vegetarian couscous or one including meat. A side salad consisting of tomatoes, cucumber, onions and avocados as well as tasty dips completed the meal. Traditionally, couscous is not eaten with cutlery but instead with your fingers. Everyone dipped and cleaned their fingers prior to dinner in small water bowls, using small towels to dry them. Three fingers of the right hand are used to form a little ball from the semolina, which is then dipped into a sauce to render it sticky for the next ingredients. Then the ball is dipped into meat or vegetables, and finally it is popped into the mouth. We took our time eating, and during the meal I tried to find out as much as possible about my two new friends, their life and of course Morocco.

Both women were in their late twenties and had been friends for a long time. They were both daughters from wealthy families which had enabled them to study at French and British universities. Now they were leading independent and successful lives. Sfia owned a small design and fashion label, and she was just about to start selling her products to France and Spain. Fatima worked in the IT business as a product developer and was part of the management of an international software company. Both told me that family was very important to them – as it was to all female Moroccans – and that they were very close to their families; however, they refused to marry unless they found men who appreciated and respected their professions and independence. They wanted to be sure that their husbands did not sit around idly at their expense, or even more worryingly that they might turn violent as was still often the case unfortunately.

I asked them if I was correct in assuming that Morocco's independence from the French protectorate in the fifties had created an atmosphere of optimism and advancement, but that nothing much had happened since. They confirmed my suspicion but opined that the young royal couple was much more consistent and resolute. They told me about an important signal that young king Mohammed VI had given, when he took over from his father Hassan II in 1999. One of his first official acts was to make changes in the palace. He dissolved his father's harem where his mother had lived with approximately another twenty women and even some of his grandfather's concubines. He also ordered his car convoy to stop at red traffic lights – something that had been previously unheard of for monarchs. In his first official speech he promised to rule using actively social politics. And, they continued, he actually did further many matters such as alphabetisation, creating new jobs and executing reforms. Soon after taking office he fired the powerful home secretary who had been controlling police, secret service and the media for more than a quarter of a century. He asked opposition members who lived abroad to return to Morocco and appointed a committee for equality and reconciliation to compensate victims of political suppression and torture. The police schools actually taught human rights these days.

The most important reform for women in Morocco had been women's equality in 2003. The king had been very ingenious, and he had even won over the conservative men in his parliament. The marriageable age had been raised to eighteen years in a legally binding 'Family Code'. Polygamy was only permitted under very restricted conditions. Women received protection from domestic violence and the right to maintenance after a divorce. Even sole custody of children was possible. They told me proudly that Mohammed VI had declared: "Morocco's future lies in the hand of our women." Since then Morocco boasted the most modern female rights in the Muslim world. Of course, it would take some time before all these rights would take root in everyday life, but Moroccan society had considerably changed since then. More and more women – just like themselves – worked in shops, hotels and in administrations, instead of looking after husband and household. A third of them were doctors, a fifth engineers and a fourth of all professors were also women. They claimed their freedom by owning small cars, and due to their work, they were able to afford them.

The king himself also led a very modern personal life. In 2002 he married the computer scientist Salma Bennani, who didn't hide her red coloured hair beneath a headscarf and wore it long. The royal couple had been blessed with a son and a daughter, and their births had been enthusiastically celebrated by the Moroccans. The younger generation looked upon him like some kind of star and affectionately called him 'M6'. During his public appearances, he often wore designer sunglasses, he drove a sports car, rode a jet ski, and he invited musicians who were idols to young Moroccans to his palace for private concerts. So his behaviour and manner aroused a lot of admiration. Despite all that, poverty and a severe lack of infrastructure remained predominant problems in the country. Every fifth Moroccan had to survive on less than £1 a day, and only about forty percent of the population had access to clean drinking water. The country also battled against terrorism, drug dealing and illegal immigration. But life had improved for the more than 30 million inhabitants of Morocco. The young king was not feared by the people like his father had been. Instead, he was admired and even loved, the ladies finished their explanations.

We had been engrossed in our conversation and had hardly noticed the musicians. Enthusiastic applause prompted us to listen more closely for a while, before continuing with our conversation. We found that the problems regarding the population development of our countries were contrasting. 65 percent of Morocco's population was younger than 18 years of age, whereas more and more old people lived in our country, which caused increasing problems due to exploding costs. An increasing number of people who no longer worked faced a decreasing number of people still earning. So Morocco should be facing a bright future considering all the young people, I mused. But the two Moroccan ladies argued that the increasing number of young Moroccans didn't find any work despite all their best efforts and that most of them didn't have a good education. Therefore, Marrakesh was faced with the paradox situation that investments in the tourist sector were increasing – a further 6,500 hotel beds were supposed to be added until 2015, bringing the total up to 100,000 – yet a properly educated work force which was required for that endeavour didn't exist. The ladies had no idea how the city council intended to deal with that dilemma.

I told them about the large building site we had discovered in the medina and asked them if they knew any more about that. They told me that an investor from Berlin was building a centre for Creativity and Congresses there. They added that the citizens of Marrakesh appreciated all the money and the new ideas that people from abroad brought to their city because it supported the spirit of optimism and advancement; however, there were also doubts whether the medina's unique magical charm which had prevailed throughout the centuries, attracting countless people from all over the world might be lost in the process. They told me about a travel report from the 14th century describing the Jemaa el-Fnaa and everything had been exactly as it was today. Similar reports and excerpts from books that spanned several centuries had been rediscovered only recently. I could understand their reservations and tried reassuring them by reminding them of last night's festivities, during which I had sensed immense respect and love for this city among the guests. That experience made me believe in the strength of Marrakesh and its ability to defend itself from losing its integrity. When I thought about my words later I wondered whether it had been my place to make such a statement, or whether I had simply been captivated by the enchanting city of Marrakesh.

After our discussion dinner was coming to an end. Tea and bowls with fresh fruit, and biscuits made from honey, dates and almonds were being served. The band played increasingly enthusiastic songs, and we turned our attention to the music. I had never heard anything like it. The group combined typical Oriental rhythms with rock music, and two women and men sang passionate songs. The women in attendance were delighted, and I found myself going with the flow. During a very rhythmic and fast piece of music, the water jets from the fountains shot up exceptionally high, and sparklers were lit in addition to the torches, spreading little glowing stars everywhere. I thought that this was the highlight of the evening but I was to be proven wrong.

The band stopped playing abruptly after the last song. There were no encores, and a pause ensued. The water jets were reduced to a quiet gentle splashing, and we saw people being busy in the catering rooms. Sfia and Fatima turned all mysterious and announced that now the main attraction of the night was about to begin. They added that the sociologist and writer Farima Mernissi had described the events that would follow now very well in one of her books. Several guests were already leaving the event nonetheless. We sat at our table in a dreamy mood and talked a little more about Marrakesh.

They told me that two writers from Marrakesh, Peter Mayne and Elias Canetti, had made the city famous after the protectorate had come to an end. Several rich people from Europe and the USA such as Paul Getty and Arndt von Bohlen and Halbach had also discovered Marrakesh in the 1960s, and they had used it as their fourth or fifth home. International jet setters as well as movie stars and pop stars visited the city for concerts or festivals. On top of the list were artists such as Andy Warhol, Bob Dylan, Leonhard Cohen, Frank Zappa, Jimi Hendrix and the Rolling Stones. Later, swarms of hippies had arrived and had raided the freely available hashish. In the mid-seventies, the king had to take action against the open selling and use of drugs – not least because the European Union and the USA put pressure on him – and drove off the hippy movement. All that notwithstanding Marrakesh still held a great appeal to people looking for new inspiration, or those wanting to learn more about the Orient's magical atmosphere. Not least the movie studios that had settled in Quarzazate, the three golf courses and the exquisite luxury hotels frequently attracted celebrities and rich people. The city council actively supported international festivals and congresses as well as traditional events and spectacles throughout the year to create tourist attractions. Today's event, however, was aimed at local women, and they had invited me because they were under the impression that I was truly interested and open for life in their city. I was flattered and curious at the same time.

About half an hour later the noise of drums sounded in the rooms that had been used for catering so far. My female companions asked me to follow them to these rooms. They were dimly lit and all I could see was a group of black drummers on the left hand side. The three rooms that were connected to each other were empty bar several benches along the walls. Many women sat crowded together on these benches, some stood beside them. Tea, fruit juice and water were being offered. The women talked quietly, some swayed to the rhythm of the music. The music gradually increased in volume and speed, and more and more women joined the movements of the others. There were hardly any interruptions between the pieces of music. Sometimes, two or three of the musicians would leave while the others continued to drum. That way they alternated in order to play without interruptions. As the drumming became faster, so did the dancing of the women. Many got up from the benches, took off their shoes, or even discarded their headscarves. Sfia and Fatima also started dancing and I let myself be drawn in. There was no pressure. Every woman could join the dance or simply sit there, watching. Some danced excessively and slumped down onto the floor after a while, dazed. Other women came along, helping them back onto one of the benches so they could rest. Later, the women threw themselves back in the fray. Everything happened as a matter of course, and I sensed that these women relieved themselves of their burdens through their dancing.

All this went on for hours. The musicians played in waves – sometimes faster, sometimes slowing down – and everybody continued to dance. I had never encountered anything like this before, not even during our beat evenings in the youth club. I immersed myself into this stream of movement and energy and felt as one with the other women. It was an everlasting swaying and surging, sometimes with our eyes closed, and I sang along with the other women although I didn't understand the words and simply went along with phonetics. The smell of cinnamon, vanilla and bergamot hovered above our heads, and rose water was being sprayed down on us to cool us down a little. All these scents increased the magical atmosphere. The more I danced, the more I forgot everything around me – time and space – and I felt my own body very intensely. Later I felt that I had reached a completely new sphere beyond my body, as if I had crossed a border. I was in ecstasy, feeling an unbridled energy. I had become one with everything and had gained another stage of consciousness, an understanding of the universe. I had an incredible feeling during the constant moving and swaying, and I could have stayed like this forever.

After a while – I think it might have been hours – the music slowly died down and finally faded. The women's movement also slowed down, and we let our dancing slowly come to an end. I hadn't seen my Moroccan friends for a while but they came over to me, hugged me, and I felt an incredible unity with them without saying a word. Just like the other women we stood a while in the centre of the room and enjoyed this feeling. Slowly, we got ready to go home. When we entered the courtyard all the torches had burned out but it had been fairly dark in the rooms so we found our way quite easily. At the exit all women received a small bottle of perfume called 'Soir de Marrakech'. I still keep it, and sometimes I open it just for a quick scent to bring back the memories.

When we left the El Badi Palace it suddenly occurred that I had not given any thought to transport for getting back home. My friends insisted on taking me back to my hotel, so we made our way through the nocturnal medina towards the Riad. We were all still captivated by the emotions we had felt during the past few hours and didn't speak at all, yet the sense of belonging prevailed. Just before we reached the Riad, the muezzins' morning prayers began. That enhanced the magic of this night, and everything felt supernatural to me.

Sfia and Fatima had asked the Riad's night porter to order a taxi for them, and together we awaited the arrival of the taxi in the same mood as before. We said a heartfelt goodbye, and I was very grateful to them for the night's experience. After they had left, I sat for quite a while on the comfortable furniture in the inner yard. I simply allowed my thoughts to come and go until I had eased gently back to something closer to reality. I disconnected from reality again, just like I had done during the dance, and felt a sense of completeness, pleasure, satisfaction and calmness in my body and soul that I could not put into words. Somehow I understood all the complexities of life and the world. I sat there for a long time until the singing of the birds in the trees startled me. Eventually, I went back to our hotel room and just as I had fallen asleep, Marianne woke me up for breakfast.

Marianne woke me pretty abruptly this morning. She had her heart set on taking me to the golf course along with her English friends. Jack and Ted had been playing on various golf courses throughout Marrakesh in the past few days, and they wanted to let us be a part of this experience because they deemed it very special. I felt very weak because I hadn't slept much but the energy from the night before returned quickly so I agreed to go to the golf course after breakfast.

After we had finished our breakfast we went from the Riad past the Lycée Mohamed V to the Bab Ghemat. Outside this city wall gate is a big square where tiny city taxis, larger overland taxis, city buses and horse-drawn carriages wait for passengers. A small merry-go-round was next to them, and everywhere, merchants began setting up their stalls with oranges, pomegranates and figs. Several cigarette dealers had also arrived at their stalls. Groups of people stood next to the road waiting for cars. We joined the queue, and when it was our turn we climbed into a taxi that took us to the golf course.

I hadn't had any previous experience with golf because neither I nor my husband had the copious amounts of time that those people we knew who played golf spent indulging in this sport, enhancing their abilities. But it was interesting, and I wondered what kind of experiences were waiting for us on a golf course in Marrakesh. Jack and Ted enthused about how they had been playing golf for years, and that they used their short holidays to play on the most wonderful golf courses of the world. As the heat became very intense on the open golf courses from midday onwards, the two men tended to start playing early in the morning. All of the golf facilities were situated outside the city, our companions told us. One of them was located in a wonderfully arranged area of the Palmerai, and two others were hidden behind large walls along the outward roads. On this particular morning we were headed towards the Royal Golf Club which could be found along the road leading towards the Atlas Mountains. First we passed a dry river bed to our left. On the far side we saw an extended city district outside of the historic town centre consisting of several old blocks of houses. We saw how the daily work was just about to begin there. Next we passed olive and fruit tree plantations where water streamed along ditches between the rows of trees. Most of the traffic on our road rushed towards the city. Suddenly we stopped by a high wall next to a large driveway. We noticed a Moroccan flag before our taxi took us to the club's reception building.

Our companions handled the formalities for playing on the golf course, grabbed their golf clubs and the other necessary accessories, and explained the characteristics of this course to us. Marianne and I only intended to accompany them part of the way, and then we wanted to enjoy the relaxation facilities for the rest of the day. The two men hadn't been able to persuade us to a trial day playing golf. When we emerged from the club house we encountered a breathtaking view. In front of us was an exquisite, cultivated lawn area with green knolls, palm trees and water ponds. Scattered throughout the landscape we saw small buildings in the familiar Moroccan style made from red clay. Beyond this extensive green spot in the middle of the desert that shone like an emerald, rose the gigantic Atlas Mountains, basking in the morning sun. We were speechless and stared at the beautiful spectacle. Marianne and I wondered whether this panorama distracted the golf players. Jack and Ted said that the golf courses in Marrakesh were definitely beautiful, but the international golf courses competed for the most beautiful facilities in the most exposed areas, so real golf enthusiasts would only regard that as a nice extra because actually playing would always first and foremost.

As promised, Marianne and I followed the two players for about an hour, but then we withdrew to a sheltered terrace overgrown with bougainvilleas near one of the golf club's casinos to relax and leave all our cares behind. We had a little snack and drank chilled non-alcoholic cocktails.

I told Marianne about the boisterous party I had attended the night before, and that there hadn't been a drop of alcohol involved. That made it an even more incredible experience considering the public drinking sprees and excesses in Europe, America and Russia that we had heard about and witnessed on more than one occasion.

Later we moved to some deckchairs on the lawn in front of the terrace and got comfortable. I even managed to catch up on some much needed sleep. In the early hours of the afternoon, just before the two golfers rejoined us again, my mobile phone rang, and André and Simone invited me and my friends for the evening to a starlit night in the desert. It took a bit of persuasion before the others agreed to come along, but they finally yielded and we arranged to meet that evening in the large square outside the Bab Ghemat.

The Englishmen wanted to show us something else special and acted all mysterious when we climbed into the taxi. Instead of heading towards town, we took off into the other direction. Approximately three kilometres away from the entrance to the golf club, the taxi driver turned left through a large gate into a fenced in area. A broad driveway led from the gate houses to a large building complex. Next to all the noble black cars in the car park our little old yellow ochre taxi seemed very humble. We left the taxi and received a very warm welcome at the hotel entrance. Apparently, we had arrived at one of the most exclusive hotels in all of Marrakesh, the Amanjena. Our companions wanted to invite us for tea here and told us that it was customary for some visitors of Marrakesh to go to one of the big noble hotel bars just to have tea. That way they could catch a glimpse of the privileged way of life, even if they couldn't afford to stay there. At first, we walked around for a bit to take in the tasteful and elegant hotel complex.

We saw a main building and several detached buildings next to a large water basin. A number of canals intersected and ran from it. The style of the buildings seemed to be a mixture of Indian and Oriental fashions. The outer and inner walls consisted of red sandstones. Large palm trees grew next to the water basins and the canals, reflecting the calm water. Neatly cut, waist-high boxwood hedges separated the areas. To the right behind the building was a large swimming pool surrounded by white tables and deckchairs beneath large white canvas shelters. The restaurant was behind that area. Turning left from the lobby, we could enter a library where guests could borrow books, music cassettes or CDs.

After admiring the neat complex, we sat down in some very comfortable seating furniture next to a small table, enjoying the wonderful view of the water basin. This room was also very tastefully decorated. Some of the first-class hotels of this chain were cluttered, but the design here was almost spartan, concentrating on unique pieces of furniture and exotic exhibits, which gave everything a tranquil and sublime tenor. By the entrance outside the lobby was a long corridor connecting the various sections of the main building. We ordered non-alcoholic cocktails and some snacks while enjoying the calm and friendly atmosphere. We felt as if a celebrity could walk in at any moment, or one of the big industrialists who were causing global sensations by buying other companies. But even if one of them had walked in, the distinguished atmosphere would have prevented us or any of the other guests from causing a stir or paying undue attention to them.

We asked one of the friendly employees what the hotel had to offer and she fetched a hotel manageress. She told us that the buildings near the basins offered complete seclusion with every conceivable comfort, and that even large with families and their entourages could stay there.

All the luxury impressed us, but also the fact that this luxury was neither pompous nor in-your-face; instead, it was quiet and subtle. In sharp contrast to all the dust, dirt and rush on the streets outside the hotel complex, everything here was painstakingly clean and extremely quiet. Once again I found these contrasts so very close to each other, like they were in no other country.

We ordered a taxi for our way back to the Riad, and once we reached the city, we walked back to the hotel from the large taxi stand at the Bab Ghemat through the historic town centre. The merry-go-round was still in action, and all sorts of knick-knacks were being sold at some booths that reminded me of our fun fairs at home. Right next to these booths we saw vegetables and fruit being sold from carts, while the nags and donkeys looked on. Everything felt so familiar, as if I had been living in this city for a long time.

At the end of this quiet day, we slowly got ready for our starlit night in the desert. We had no idea what awaited us, and we assumed that it would get cold outside as there were no buildings to store and emit the heat of the day. So Marianne and I put some jeans on and wore jumpers over our blouses. We also took blazers and warm scarves.

At eight o'clock sharp all four of us arrived at the car park, but I didn't find my French friends. We walked around between the countless groups of people with heavy luggage waiting at the taxi stand, and finally I spotted them at the left end of the square, waving. They had brought a mini bus and had been looking for us as well. A young Swiss couple also tagged along. Once we had climbed aboard, the driver pulled away sharply. He took the same route towards the Atlas Mountains that we had used this morning to reach the golf course. André and Simone told us that the taxi stand at Bab Ghemat was the meeting point for city sightseeing tours, as well as excursions to Quarzazate and into the Atlas Mountains. They also explained that the service of the small yellow ochre taxis was limited to sightseeing trips through the city, whereas the larger crème-coloured taxis also took passengers to the airport or out into the countryside. That explained the large number of people, as people from the Atlas or other areas further away would meet here to make their long journey back home after they had finished running their errands or selling their wares, which they had previously brought to Marrakesh. Usually it would take them well into the night or even until the next day to get home. That was one of the reasons why the square was permanently busy.

They also told us more about the city districts on the far side of the dry riverbed. The closely spaced houses were not quite as old as the medina. This part of the city was closer to the city centre than all the new districts with their modern flats that had been built around Marrakesh, and which we had seen during our sightseeing tour.

We passed the golf club and the driveway that led to the Amanjena and carried on along that road towards the Atlas Mountains for another 45 minutes. Eventually the driver turned right, following a bumpy road through a barren landscape for several kilometres. Finally we stopped outside a flat, fenced in compound. Many other cars were already parked here. When we left the taxi, dusk was already fading into darkness. Passing through a large wooden gate we saw uncountable small lights dotted all over the compound.

On the far side we noticed a large tent that was open on three sides. In front of it was an open area. Several small clay structures stood to the left and the right of the tent, containing red embers and emitting some smoke. Next to those were more tents, although somewhat smaller than the first one. Inside, people were busy with pots, pans and drinks.

After we had a chance to look around, André asked where we wanted to settle down, so we headed towards one of the small lights towards the front on the right hand side. All I could see was that these small lights were little oil lamps standing on very low round wooden tables. Large sitting cushions and woollen blankets had been scattered around these tables. Settling down on the comfortable cushions at our table, we made some jokes about the unusual seating position. We awaited the rest of the evening curiously. We were told that we would be eating mechoui – a whole lamb roasted in a clay oven – the most popular Moroccan feast. Before roasting, the lamb is prepared with concentrated butter and onions, put on a spit and placed in a small, specially built clay oven: the little structures we had noticed to the left and the right of the large tent. Prior to placing the lamb inside, those ovens will be filled with glowing coals for hours to ensure that they are piping hot. Once the lamb is inside, the oven will be sealed with clay. After several hours the oven will be opened again. The timing has to be perfect as the meat of the lamb is supposed to be extremely tender, but the skin must turn out to be crisp and golden. We assumed that we would have to wait for a while longer but were pleasantly surprised to learn that dinner was to be served shortly after the music had started playing in the big tent and we had received some chilled orange juice.

Our seats were at the front, and in the light of the torches we were able to watch the catering personnel opening the clay ovens, extracting the steaming lambs and placing the spits on mountings. They carved the lambs with large knives that looked almost like sabres, placing the pieces on large platters. The delicious smell of the meat wafted across the whole area, and our mouths were watering in anticipation.

The platters were distributed amongst the tables, along with flatbread, pickled olives and other vegetables preserved in oil and herbs. We were all absolutely delighted. The meat was indeed very tender, the flatbread had been freshly baked and the aromatic side dishes were sensational. We kept helping ourselves to more. The French couple had brought along four bottles of red wine because they thought that such a delicacy would taste three times better if accompanied by a good red wine. Since alcohol was not offered at these feasts due to Islamic tradition, people would bring their own wine, and the hosts both understanding and gracious in allowing it.

During the almost two hours while we were eating we had hardly noticed the music. Now, a band of musicians played Oriental music under the large tent, and a young man and woman sang. The melody was very catchy. It sounded like a love song or some kind of passionate debate. I obviously didn't understand a word of the song, but the word 'asni' or 'asi' was frequently repeated. The song completely lulled me, and I began humming along. Another two songs later, belly dancers began a performance on the empty area outside the tent. This area was partially illuminated by torches, which added to the magical atmosphere that the movements of the dancers were creating. I felt as if I was in a fairytale.

At first, the dance and the music were slow, but gradually the rhythm of the music increased, and the graceful movement of the dancers became more expressive. Towards the end, the rendition reached a climax, and all artists exuded ecstasy. They sang, danced and the audience was completely drawn in. More and more spectators ran to the dance floor and joined in, and we also got carried away. When the performance came to an end, we were in each other's arms, full of enthusiasm.

A pause ensued, and we talked about the music and the dancing. Simone told us that this particular band was extremely popular in Morocco, and that the belly dancers had become famous due to their performances in one of the night clubs in Marrakesh. After about half an hour without music, we were asked to douse the oil lamps on our tables. All the torches had already burnt down in the meantime. Complete darkness fell over the area. When we looked around and up, we saw a breathtaking picture: above us, tantalising and almost within our reach, we saw the stars. The sky was full of stars. They glowed brightly, and I had never seen so many stars in Europe before. Everyone at the table shared this notion, and all the other guests were equally overwhelmed and couldn't avert their eyes. We looked for constellations, whispering to each other when we recognised something. Above the stars we noticed a white misty band – the Milky Way was also clearly visible here.

Once the initial awe had passed, we felt humbled and reverent. It was then that we realised what a starlit night in the desert really meant. André said that they had seen this night sky in the desert many times, but that it still overwhelmed them each and every time they saw it.

After a long silence our hosts asked their audience for their attention in French and Arabic. They announced that everyone could choose a star from the night sky, and that a particular star would be designated to them. This designation would be registered, and we would receive a certificate. Several large telescopes had been placed around the dancing area, and everyone could peer through them to pick their star. I was all giddy with excitement about this prospect and was one of the first to sign in for the registration. When I peered through the telescope, all the stars seemed even closer and clearer. I watched them gleaming and sparkling. I took a long time to choose a particular star. What criteria should I use to pick one or the other? While I was still searching my mysterious female friend from Marrakesh approached me. I hadn't seen her here tonight yet. She greeted me warmly, chose a star together with me, and we talked a little about my stay in Marrakesh. With her assistance I decided on a small star near the constellation Delphinus, and received my registration certificate with the number 169979. I told her that I would be leaving Marrakesh on the following day, and she promised that she would come to the airport. She also said that she was eager to find out about my personal secret.

It took a long time before everyone had registered their stars, but I wasn't bored at all because it was just as exciting watching the others choosing their stars as it had been chosen my own. Everyone on our table selected their stars one by one, and finally, we received our registration certificates. Marianne and Jack took a joint registration, and this small gesture was a wonderful token of their new love. While the designations were being registered, the musicians had begun playing drums quietly. Once all the guests had received their star certificates and the telescopes had been taken away, the band took to the stage again, increasing the volume and speed of their music. The drummers began singing songs, and some spectators joined in. More and more people took to the dance floor, dancing in circles. We also joined them and danced until we noticed that people were heading out to leave. Eventually we signalled that it was time for us to head back to Marrakesh as well.

In the car we talked almost the entire time about this astonishing night, and we were all proud of our respective stars. When we approached Marrakesh, the new day was already dawning on the horizon, and Marianne and I knew that we had to fly home at lunchtime. I wasn't tired although I hadn't slept all night; instead, I was still captivated by the magic of the events.

The Swiss couple persuaded me to get changed quickly in my hotel and meet them back at the Bab Ghemat for a jogging session along the twelve kilometre long city wall. They told me that they had done this several times already, since they frequently visited Marrakesh. They insisted this was a wonderful experience when the city was still asleep and not quite so hot.

At half past four the muezzins began their morning prayers, and we slowly trotted along the city wall in a western direction, anti-clockwise so to speak. At this time of day there was none of the hustle and bustle on the roads or in the medina. Only a few cars drove along the wide roads outside of the historic city centre, and a convoy of the waste collection service set off in their large wagons. So far, I had only seen sections of the city wall during our sightseeing tours, while we were in a taxi, or when we left the historic city centre through one of the gates. Now I saw it in all its glory, and I could easily imagine what the people had felt hundreds of years ago, and even today, when they sought shelter within. That warm red colour increasing in intensity as the sun rose, heightened the feeling of being safe behind this wall.

At the south-western part of the city wall we took a turn and ran along the Rue de la Menara until we reached the Menara gardens. They were already open, and the irrigation ditches were just being flooded. We circled around the large water basin, admiring the reflection of the small pavilion that one of the previous sultans had built here for his favoured wife, and ran up and down several paths in the orchards, before heading back to the Rue and the city wall. We had been out running for two hours, and my jogging partners said goodbye when we arrived at the Riad. I thanked them for this wonderful experience, made my way back to my room, and fell into a sound sleep until ten o'clock.

I gulped down my breakfast. Marianne had been awake a while longer and had said goodbye to her new love. Jack and Ted had to head for the airport earlier than we did, and time was of the essence after the long night. We quickly packed our belongings, and we decided to take one last walk across the Jemaa el-Fnaa. It was just after 11am when we set off through the narrow alleys. Life was already pretty hectic here at this time of day; tourists were out and about, and locals were going about their business.

We circled the square once, and then settled down for one last coffee on the terrace of the Café de France. Deep in thought we recalled the previous days. Smiling, we said goodbye and returned to the hotel where the taxi to the airport would pick us up. When we arrived at the hotel to begin our journey home, I received the news that my suitcase had arrived at the airport in Marrakesh. It had been misdirected, and my missing item report at the airport had been successful in the end. I picked it up at the service desk before leaving and took it back home, unopened.

A New Life Begins

The plane landed with a jolt. I had fallen asleep just after take-off in Madrid, so this was a bumpy landing in more ways than one. I rubbed my eyes, not knowing where I was. While the plane rolled slowly from the runway to the gate, the other passengers rose, dragging their luggage from the compartments. Neither Marianne nor I made any visible effort to get up. Marianne was still thinking about her new love, and I still found it difficult to absorb the fact that I would be home soon. It seemed a lifetime away after all of my new and incredible experiences and sensations of the last few days. We mechanically completed the remainder of the journey back to our respective flats. As we were still preoccupied with our feelings and also exceedingly tired, we said a quick goodbye and parted ways.

My husband wasn't home when I arrived, so I sat down in our kitchen, brewed a cup of tea and sipped it slowly. I looked around and everything was the same as before my trip to Marrakesh. And yet it was also different. Something must have happened during the six days I had been away. I felt both at home and a stranger at the same time. Smells, noises and colours were very intensive and transformed into emotions. It was as if I felt and sensed everything that I saw and heard. I had never perceived my surroundings in such an intensive way. My senses truly were tingling.

I got restless after a while and unpacked my suitcase, laboriously packing all my items away. Finally, late at night, my husband came home. We were overjoyed to see each other. It felt as if we had been separated for years and had only just found each other again. We went to bed soon after, and for the first time in a long while we enjoyed some tenderness and passion. I slept long and sound afterwards.

At breakfast the next morning my husband fixed me with his gaze and asked: "What's the matter? You are completely changed! Did you really go to Marrakesh, or did you go somewhere else? Tell me about your experiences and what you've been up to".

I replied: "Of course I was in Marrakesh, what gives you the idea that I have done anything else?" He answered: "You seem to have undergone some kind of beauty treatment or rejuvenation cure. You are radiant. How did you do that?" There was only one answer to that: "We had some rather intensive days. I encountered many new experiences, and got to know a completely different world. But I can't talk about it just yet. I'm not able to put into words all that I have seen, heard, smelled and felt. I need to digest all those things first myself, and I can't do that by talking about it. Please accept that". He looked at me incredulously, his gaze intensifying. So I added: "Rest assured that it didn't involve another man, and it hasn't got anything to do with Marianne either. This is just about me". He relaxed visibly: "That sounds almost magical!"

Work caught up with me very fast during the next couple of days. But the new state of mind prevailed. I was confronted with emotions and feelings during conversations and various tasks that I had never noticed before. For the first time

I seemed to be open for something that I had apparently pushed away before travelling to Marrakesh. I wondered whether I had been jaded or dead inside before my holiday.

Sometimes, I was under the impression that I was able to perceive what other people thought or felt. There were even moments when someone else's words had already formed in my mind, before that person had spoken them out loud. My conversation partners or people that I had met only by accident voiced thoughts I had already formed.

On occasion I felt a sudden surge of warmth or a chill in my body, which made me pay special attention to what my counterpart was saying, or to events in my immediate surroundings. These sensations were all new; so far in similar situations, I had been focused but without emotions. Before my trip to Morocco everything happened within my mind; now, my body also participated. I realised with increasing clarity that all my senses had been enhanced, and that they were exceptionally receptive. Undoubtedly, Marrakesh had changed me – for the better.

There was one thing though that didn't let me rest. I had no explanation why my mysterious friend, whom I had met so frequently in Marrakesh, had failed to show up at the airport despite her promise. I had no contact number and no address, so I was unable to look for her or contact her from home. It bothered me that I had not discovered this personal secret that she had told me about so emphatically. I became increasingly restless because I couldn't find this secret, despite all the changes that my husband admired on a daily basis which changed our lives, making them very intense again.

Three months later I awoke in the middle of the night. The restlessness that had befallen me before my dreamless sleep still prevailed, and it had taken over my entire body. I sat up in bed, propped myself against the headrest and stared into the darkness. Suddenly it hit me, an emotion, an epiphany, a deep and profound understanding. Warmth and light washed over my body, despite the darkness that surrounded me.

Suddenly I knew what my personal secret about Marrakesh was: *Marrakesh is the past, the present and the future all at once.* And I have experienced everything at the same time.

I followed that thought and developed this insight further, and it all became clear to me. Those six days in Marrakesh had been exactly that – past, present and future. The light of the star had come from the past when I beheld that glorious night, and it will still be there in the future. My mysterious friend was another me – and my other self from the future had accompanied me during my visit to Marrakesh in the present. That was the reason why she couldn't come to the airport, because when I left the city during the present, she reverted back to being the future. I could only live through these experiences and feelings during my visit in Marrakesh, because the intensity of life in this city had opened my mind to and allowed me to be receptive to this phenomenon.